Ezra Asher Cook

Knights of Pythias Illustrated

Ezra Asher Cook

Knights of Pythias Illustrated

ISBN/EAN: 9783337286781

Printed in Europe, USA, Canada, Australia, Japan

Cover: Foto ©Andreas Hilbeck / pixelio.de

More available books at **www.hansebooks.com**

KNIGHTS OF PYTHIAS

ILLUSTRATED

𝕬 𝕱𝖚𝖑𝖑 𝕴𝖑𝖑𝖚𝖘𝖙𝖗𝖆𝖙𝖊𝖉 𝕰𝖝𝖕𝖔𝖘𝖎𝖙𝖎𝖔𝖓

OF THE

CEREMONIES OF THE THREE DEGREES

OF THE

SUBORDINATE LODGE.

REVISED EDITION.

7.0722 ℒ.

—————— •◦•✠•◦• ——————

CHICAGO, ILL.

EZRA A. COOK & CO., PUBLISHERS.

1878.

TABLE OF CONTENTS.

PUBLISHERS' PREFACE.

"At the devil's booth are all things sold;
Each ounce of dross costs its ounce of gold.
For a cap and bells our lives we pay,
Bubbles we earn with a whole soul's tasking,
'Tis heaven alone that is given away:
'Tis only God may be had for the asking."

LOWELL.

Little did we think, when reading in youth, of the follies, false methods and narrow views of the Knighthood of the "Dark Ages" so truthfully caricatured in the History of Don Quixote; mentally contrasting them with Christian civilization founded on the Holy Bible; that in our time in our own land an army of Knights more foolish, blind and guilty than those burlesqued by Don Quixote would voluntarily enroll their names and parade the streets of our cities.

Like Masonry and Odd Fellowship, this order makes use of the Bible but like the former it puts the implements of the order on top of the Bible (the first rank excepted.) The fact that the very name "Book of Law" is the term which the great apostle of Masonry, Albert G. Mackey applies to the sacred book on the altar which he says: "is that volume which by the religion of the country is believed to contain the revealed will of the Grand Architect of the universe," (Mackey's Jurisprudence p. 33,) gives good reason for the conclusion that this term was chosen in order that the Bible may be conveniently replaced by any other sacred book when the order is established in heathen or Mohamedan countries.

HISTORICAL SKETCH OF THE KNIGHTS OF PYTHIAS.

This secret order which now claims a membership of 100,000 and whose supreme council of the world "composed only of Officers and Ex-Officers of Grand Lodges, which Aug. 14th, 1877, met in Cleveland, Ohio, about 2,000 strong, had its origin in the fertile brain of an ambitious adventurer by the name of J. H. Rathbone. As of the Grange, Washington, D. C., was its birth place and Washington Lodge No. 1, was formally organized Feb. 23d, 1864, though a preliminary meeting for the purpose was held the 19th, four days before. The ritual prepared previously by J. H. Rathbone, was adopted and a committee was appointed to prepare an addition thereto with Rathbone as Chairman. In four days more they met again adopted the additional ritual and appointed a committee to prepare still more ritual which with some revisions formed the three Ranks of the order. March 24th, steps were taken to organize a Grand Lodge, and April 8th, the Grand Lodge of the District of Columbia was organized and they were ready to sell Secrets at wholesale and retail.

Whether the founder of the order, J. H. Rathbone, had expected to have the monopoly of the business of selling the Secrets of the order or not he seems to have been displeased at the formation or perhaps the management of the Grand Lodge, for he resigned his office as Venerable Patriarch and even his membership in the order, but two weeks afterwards. He is soon heard of as again revising the ritual of the order.

Within four months after the organization of Washington Lodge No. 1, two other lodges had been started there and one in Alexandria, Va.

Within six months from the formation of the "Mother Lodge" it with all but one of the children were dead and the Grand Lodge also. In 1866 the members of Franklin Lodge No. 2, Washington D. C., the only surviving lodge started another lodge in the city and the Grand Lodge was also, resusitated soon after. July 1867 the total membership was still but 694, but in three months increased to 1330, and March 10th the District of Columbia Grand Lodge issued charters for the Grand Lodges of Maryland and New Jersey.

August 11th, 1868 the Supreme Grand Lodge of the world was organized at Washington D C., and at its first session afterwards at Richmond, Va., March 9th, 1869 the membership was reported at over 35,000 with nearly 200 lodges, eight Grand Lodges and an income of $194,573,25, and the year following had increased to 52,000 members, 465 lodges and sixteen Grand Lodges, the total receipt being $541,219,34, at the close of the year 1870 the membership is reported at 84,000.

With this apparent prosperity there had been some fierce wrangling, quite at variance with the great friendship the order professes to inculcate. Even the Civil Courts were several times appealed to, to decide questions of disputed authority and 1870 found two Grand Lodges in both Maryland and New Jersey and a bitter war in the Supreme Lodge of the World, on the question of Rathbone's new rank and a new Obligation ordered by the Supreme Lodge to be administered to every member of the order, which thousands refused to take.

For several years the order has been used by political tricksters nine-tenths of them high Masons to such an extent as to thorough- ly disgust its most intelligent members in many localities and its managers are forced to admit a net loss of 5,942 during the past year, while it is undoubtedly true that a very large number still reported as members will never again enter their "Castle Halls."

That this little volume may be blessed of God in the utter demolition of this dark order is the hope and prayer of

The Publishers.

DIAGRAM,

Showing the shape of the stations, which are designated in the Lodge by the following colors: Chancellor Commander, red: Vice Chancellor, blue; Prelate, black: Past Chancellor, yellow. The altar here shown is arranged for the Third or Chivalric Rank of Knight. The Initials F. C. B. shown on the shields on sides of Altar stand for the pass-words of the three ranks—**Friendship, Caution, Bravery.**

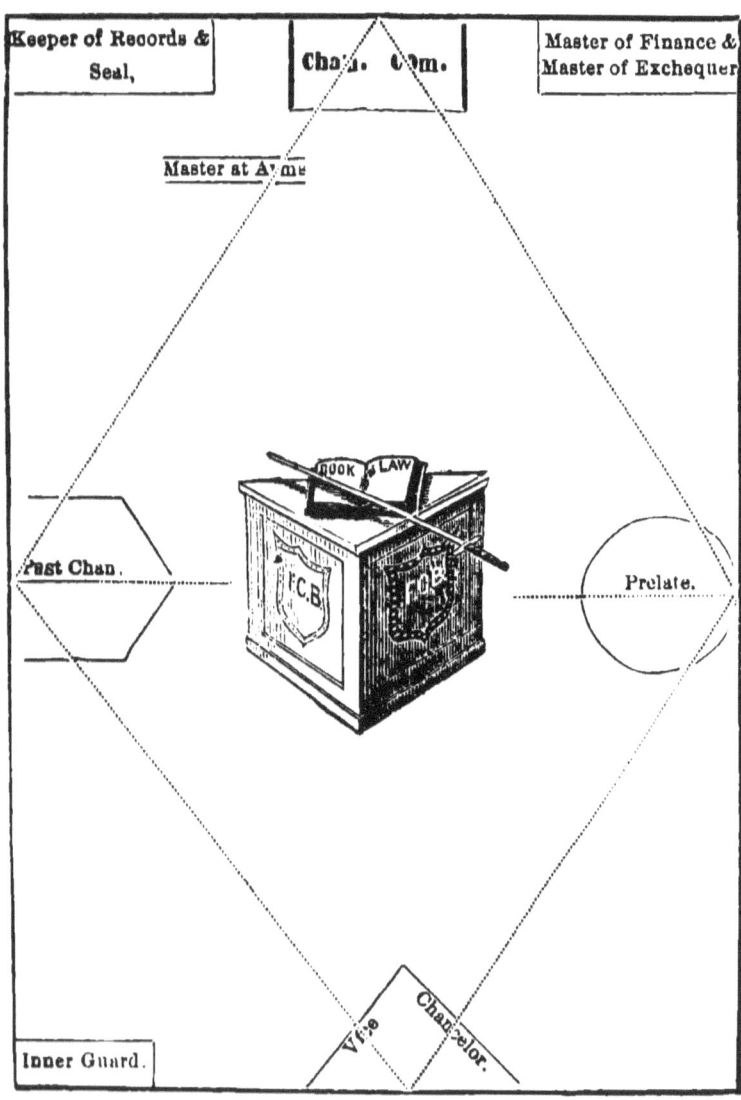

KNIGHTS OF PYTHIAS ILLUSTRATED.

QUALIFICATIONS AND TITLES OF OFFICERS.

1ST. PAST CHANCELLOR.—Acquired by service in having passed through the executive office and chair of the Lodge, and which title and rank he shall hold thereafter.

2D. CHANCELLOR COMMANDER.—Attained by election: which latter title of Commander shall only be held and worn while the principal and executive officer of the Lodge. Service as Chancellor Commander to end of term entitles to the rank of Past Chancellor ever afterwards.

3RD. VICE CHANCELLOR.—Attained by election.

4TH. PRELATE.—Attained by election.

5TH. MASTER OF EXCHEQUER.—Attained by election.

6TH. MASTER OF FINANCE.—Attained by election.

7TH. KEEPER OF RECORDS AND SEAL.—Attained by election.

8TH. MASTER AT ARMS.—By election or appointment.

9TH. INNER GUARD.—By appointment.

10TH. OUTER GUARD.—By appointment.

POSITION OF OFFICERS IN THE LODGE.

PAST CHANCELLOR.—On the right hand side of the Lodge, midway or center of room, looking from Chancellor Commander's station to the Vice Chancellor's station at the opposite end.

CHANCELLOR COMMANDER.—At the head or end of the room.

VICE CHANCELLOR.—At opposite or lower end of room.

PRELATE.—On left hand side of the Chancellor Commander, at center of the Lodge, and in a direct line as drawn from the Past Chancellor, over or through the Altar, opposite the position of the Past Chancellor.

MASTER OF EXCHEQUER, } At head of Lodge-room and on the
MASTER OF FINANCE, } left hand of the Chancellor Com.

KEEPER OF RECORDS AND SEAL, } At head of Lodge-room
MASTER AT ARMS, } and on the right of the
Chancellor Commander.

INNER GUARD.—At inner door and near the Vice Chancellor.

OUTER GUARD.—At outer door.

OPENING CEREMONIES.

At precisely the hour appointed for the convening of the Lodge, if a quorum be present, the Chancellor Commander seeing that the members are clothed in proper regalia, or insignia of the Order, and after notifying the Master at arms to satisfy himself that all present are duly qualified as members in good standing of the Order, and in possession of, and with the proper rank and Semi Annual Pass word gives one rap with his gavel or sword hilt.

Chancellor Commander.—"It is my will and pleasure that —— Lodge, No. —, Knights of Pythias, now come to order, in this 'Castle Hall,' for the dispatch of such business and work as may be brought before it. The officers and members will give me their aid and counsel in further promulgating the bonds of **Friendship** that unite us, using due **Caution** in the transaction of any business that is presented, and with **Bravery** accepting all issues which, with strict impartiality and fairness, we may be called to pass upon. Let Harmony, Peace and Unity prevail.

"Brother Inner Guard, you will order the Outer Guard to clear the ante-room, close the doors and permit no one to enter until the Lodge is duly and regularly opened, and he notified of the same through you by me."

Inner Guard to Outer Guard (opens door).—"It is the will and pleasure of the Chancellor Commander that you permit no one to enter until the Lodge is duly and regularly opened, and you are notified of the same by him through me."

Outer Guard.—"The commands of the Chancellor Commander shall be obeyed."

Inner Guard to Chancellor Commander (closes and locks inner door).—"Chancellor Commander, the Outer Guard has received your commands and will implicitly obey them."

Chancellor Commander (two raps—all rise).—"The brethren will attend while the Prelate implores the blessings of Deity."

OPENING PRAYER BY PRELATE.

"We humbly invoke Thy blessing, thou Supreme Ruler of the Universe, upon the officers and members of this Lodge. Grant, we beseech Thee, thine aid in conducting the business for which we are here assembled; and may it please Thee to shower divine grace upon us in this our convention. Let harmony and brotherly love prevail among, and finally permit us to assemble around Thy throne at the last great day, a happy and united brotherhood, elected to share Thy heavenly home. Hear, we beseech **Thee**, and answer us in peace, for Thine own sake. Amen."

(All respond.) Amen.

OPENING ODE.

Great God, to Thee we raise
Our hopeful song of praise—
Grant us Thy love.
Let us in friendship be;
Let us harmonious see,
Our Order extended be,
All nations o'er.

Let brothers hand in hand
True to each other stand
Throughout all time.
Then when life's labor's o'er,
Leaving Time's earthly shore,
May we meet to part no more
In Heaven above.

Chancellor Commander.—Three raps. (All seated.)

Chancellor Commander (one rap) "Brother Inner Guard."

Inner Guard (rising promptly).—"Chancellor Commander."

Chancellor Commander.—Brother Inner Guard, you will relieve the Brother Outer Guard and have him present himself at your station."

Inner Guard retires and relieves the Outer Guard, who immediately presents himself at the station of the Inner Guard and says:

" Chancellor Commander, the Outer Guard reports for duty."

Chancellor Commander.—" Brother Outer Guard."

Outer Guard.—"Chancellor Commander."

Chancellor Commander.—" Where is your station, and what are your duties?"

Outer Guard (standing).—" Outside of the inner, and to take charge of the outer door. My duties are to see that the brethren clothe themselves in proper regalia or insignia of the Order in the ante-room, and are duly qualified to enter the inner door; to take charge of the regalia, and perform such other duties as the Chancellor Commander may direct."

Chancellor Commander.—" Brother Outer Guard, you will now resume your proper station and relieve the Brother Inner Guard."

Inner Guard returns, assumes his station, and says:

" Chancellor Commander, the Inner Guard reports from his station."

Chancellor Commander.—" Brother Inner Guard."

Inner Guard (standing).—" Chancellor Commander."

Chancellor Commander.—" Where is your station, and what are your duties in this Lodge? "

Inner Guard.—" At the inner door near the Vice Chancellor. My duties are to allow no brother to enter the Lodge who is not clothed in proper regalia or insignia of the Order, and does not give the correct raps and pass words, and to obey such other orders as may be communicated to me by the Chancellor Commander."

(Inner Guard remains standing),

Chancellor Commander (one rap).—" Brother Master at Arms."

Master at Arms (rising promptly and facing the C. C.).—" Chancellor Commander."

Chancellor Commander.—" Where is your station and what are your duties in this Lodge? "

Master at Arms.—" At the right and in front of the Chancellor Commander. My duties are to examine all present prior to the opening of the Lodge in any rank, and report the result of said examination to the Chancellor Commander; to prepare and accompany all Retainers, Pages or Esquires during the ceremonies of initiation, proving or charging in the different grades of rank, and perform such other duties as the Chancellor Commander may direct." (Master at Arms remains standing.)

Chancellor Commander (one rap).—" Brother Keeper of Records and Seal."

Keeper of Records and Seal (standing).—" Chancellor Commander."

Chancellor Commander.—" Where is your station and what are your duties in this Lodge? "

Keeper of Records and Seal.—" At the right of the Chancellor Commander. My duties are to keep a just and impartial record of all the proceedings of this Lodge, conduct all its correspondence, have charge of the Seal and Archives, make out semi-annual returns of the work and business of this Lodge, and transmit the same to the Grand Lodge; deliver any funds, documents, or other Lodge property coming into my hands to the proper officer, and to faithfully perform all other duties prescribed by the Constitution and By-Laws of this Lodge." (Keeper of Records and Seal remains standing.)

Chancellor Commander (one rap,.—"Brother Master of Finance."

Master of Finance (standing).—"Chancellor Commander."

Chancellor Commander.—"Where is your station and what are your duties in this Lodge?"

Master of Finance.—"At the left of the Chancellor Commander. My duties are too keep an accurate account between this Lodge and its members; notify all brethren who are in arrears; receive all monies and immediately pay the same over to the Master of Exchequer, taking his receipt therefor; to make out and present to this Lodge my report at the expiration of the semi-annual term, and to perform all other duties required of me by the Constitution and Ritual of the Order." (Master of Finance remains standing.)

Chancellor Commander (one rap).—"Brother Master of Ex-chequer."

Master of Exchequer (standing).—"Chancellor Commander."

Chancellor Commander.—"Where is your station and what are your duties in this Lodge?"

Master of Exchequer.—"At the left of the Chancellor Commander. My duties are to receive from the Master of Finance all Lodge monies received by him, giving my receipt therefor, keeping an exact and true account of all monies so received, making no disbursements thereof unless authorized so to do by the Lodge under an order from the Chancellor Commander, attested by the Keeper of Records and Seal, and to make a correct report to this Lodge at the end of every semi-annual term " (Master of Exchequer remains standing.)

Chancellor Commander (one rap).—"Brother Prelate."

Prelate (standing).—"Chancellor Commander."

Chancellor Commander.—"Where is your station and what are your duties in this Lodge?"

Prelate.—"On the left of the Chancellor Commander and opposite the Altar, forming one end of the base line of the double triangle. My duties are to perform all obligatory ceremonials in the conferring of the several grades of rank; offer up invocations

to, and ask blessings from the Deity upon our labors and brotherhood, and perform such other duties required of me by the Constitution, Laws and usuages of the order, or as may be directed
from time to time by the Chancellor Commander of this Lodge."
(Prelate remains standing.)

Chancellor Commander (one rap).—" Brother Vice Chancellor."

Vice Chancellor (standing).—" Chancellor Commander."

Chancellor Commander.—" Where is your station and what are
your duties in this Lodge?"

Vice Chancellor.—" In the second official chair, forming the
apex of the second triangle, opposite to and facing the Chancellor
Commander. My duties are to have charge of the second triangle and assist the Chancellor Commander in preserving order
and decorum in the Lodge, aid in conducting the ceremonies of
the several grades of rank, appoint a minority of all committees,
(unless otherwise ordered by the Lodge,) preside in the absence
of the Chancellor Commander, and have charge of the wicket."
(Vice Chancellor remains standing.)

Chancellor Commander (one rap).—" Brother Past Chancellor."

Past Chancellor (standing).—" Chancellor Commander."

Chancellor Commander.—" Where is your station and what are
your duties in this Lodge?"

Past Chancellor.—" On the right of the Chancellor Commander,
opposite the Altar, forming the terminal of the base line of the
double triangle. My duties, to have special supervision of all
preparations and be held responsible for all floor-work or ceremonies in conferring the several grades of rank, and such other
duties as the Chancellor Commander may direct."

Chancellor Commander.—" Where is the station and what are
the duties of the Chancellor Commander of this Lodge?"

Past Chancellor.—" The station of the Chancellor Commander
is in the first official chair, forming the head of the first triangle
and Lodge. It is the duty of the Chancellor Commander to preside over and have charge of both triangles, the officers, members
and visitors of his Lodge, preserve order during its session,
appoint a majority of all committees (unless otherwise ordered
by the Lodge), decide all questions of order without debate, subject, however, to an appeal to the Lodge, and perform such other
duties appertaining to his office as may be prescribed in the
work of the Order and By-Laws of his Lodge." (Past Chancellor remains standing.)

Chancellor Commander two raps; (rising to his feet; all rise). —"All of which duties I am under solemn obligation to perform with justice and impartiality; in view of which I earnestly ask the kind co-operation of the officers and members of this Lodge. Let not anger or dissension arise in our midst, but let us devote our whole attention, our entire zeal, to the labor before us; and finally, let lessons of Obedience be inculcated, **Strength** be our motto, **Friendship** our watchword, and **Caution** our guiding star. Let harmony and peace prevail."

Chancellor Commander.—"I now declare —— Lodge, No. —, duly opened for the transaction of such business as shall legally come before it.   Brother Master at Arms, you will arrange the Altar."

(The Master at Arms goes to the Altar, opens the Book and places the swords of Defence in proper position, (see instructions for arrangement of the Altar in the different grades of rank, page 15) and returns to his place.)

Chancellor Commander (addressing Inner Guard).—"Brother Inner Guard, you will communicate to the Outer Guard that this Lodge is now open, and to admit all brethren duly qualified to enter."

Inner Guard (opens door and goes out).—"Brother Outer Guard, it is the order of the Chancellor Commander that you admit all brethren duly qualified to enter, as the Lodge is regularly opened." (Returns and shuts the door.)

Inner Guard.—"Chancellor Commander, your commands have been obeyed."

Chancellor Commander gives three raps, seating the Lodge.

ORDER OF BUSINESS.

1. Calling Roll of Officers.
2. Reading Minutes.
3. Reception of Petitions.
4. Reports of Committees.
5. Balloting for Candidates.
6. Conferring Grades of Rank.
7. Communications and Bills Read.
8. New Business.
9. Has any brother any thing to offer for the good of the Order?
10. Closing in due form.

CLOSING CEREMONIES.

Chancellor Commander.—"There being no further business* before the Lodge, we will proceed to close.   The brethren will attend while the Prelate implores the blessing of Deity on our deliberations." (Two raps.)

NOTE.—If there are candidates in waiting or other business, these closing ceremonies are deferred till the Lodge is ready to close.

CLOSING PRAYER BY THE PRELATE.

"Vouchsafe Thy blessing, our Heavenly Father, on the events of this evening. Be with us during the coming week. Shield us from all harm, and finally permit us to be with Thee on the last great day, a united brotherhood, elected to share the blessings of life eternal in the heavens. Hear and answer us in peace for Thy great name's sake. Amen."

(All respond.) Amen.

CLOSING ODE.

May your slumbers be all blest
When you close your eyes in rest;
May the holy angels keep
Vigils o'er you while you sleep.
Sleep till rosy morning comes,
With its light to bless your homes;
Bless the angels that will keep
Vigils o'er you while you sleep.
Good night.

Chancellor Commander.—"Officers and brethren, we are now about to quit these portals to mingle again with the outer world. Let all of us endeavor to so regulate our conduct that it will bring credit upon ourselves and honor to our order. In conclusion, permit me to return you my sincere thanks as Chancellor Commander, for the kind assistance you have rendered in conducting the business of this convention. And now, by virtue of the power vested in me as Chancellor Commander, I declare —— Lodge, No. ——, duly closed until our next regular convention, (except in case of necessity, when all shall receive due notice,) and then I hope to see as many of you present as can possibly make it convenient to attend."

"Brother Master at Arms, you will close the Book of Law and secure the Swords of Defense. Brother Inner Guard you will now permit the brethren to retire, and inform the Outer Guard that the lodge is closed." (One rap.)

ARRANGEMENT OF THE ALTAR IN THE DIFFERENT GRADES OF RANK.

When the Lodge is called to order by the Chancellor Commander, there will be lying upon the altar a Bible, which is closed, and resting on it will be two swords, hilts together, and handles towards the Chancellor Commander's station. When the Chancellor Commander orders the Master at Arms to "arrange the altar," he will go there and arrange it as follows:

THE ALTAR IN THE INITIATORY RANK OF PAGE.

The Book opened the same as in the Chivalric Rank of Knight, and whether on the altar or **Coffin** rests ON the two Swords, which are crossed underneath the Book, with the hilts or handles toward the Chancellor Commander and points towards the Vice Chancellor. (While initiating, the handles should be towards the Prelate and points towards the candidate.)

THE ALTAR IN THE ARMORIAL RANK OF ESQUIRE.

The Book opened, the same as in the Chivalric Rank of Knight, with the two swords laying on it—crossed—with the handles towards the Chancellor Commander and points towards the Vice Chancellor.

THE ALTAR IN THE CHIVALRIC RANK OF KNIGHT.

The Book opened about the middle so as to lay square, and ONE sword laying diagonally across and over it, with the handle—or hilt—towards the foot of the room—or Vice Chancellor's station —and point towards the head of the room, or Chancellor Commander's station.

INITIATION.

FIRST, OR INITIATORY RANK OF PAGE.

 The candidate is brought into the ante-room, and as soon as his presence is known the utmost silence must be maintained in the Lodge. The Chancellor Commander will delegate one or two members to prepare the properties, under the supervision and control of the Past Chancellor; the rest of the lodge, after clothing themselves in their **Masks and Black Robes,** remain seated. Loud talk or heavy walking must be avoided, as the solemnity of the initiation depends entirely on the strict silence that pervades the room. The Master at Arms retires to the anteroom and prepares the candidate.

PREPARATION FOR FIRST, OR INITIATORY RANK OF PAGE.

The preparation consists in the candidate having his coat and vest removed, the **White Robe** put on and his eyes securely blindfolded, in which manner he is conducted to the door of the Lodge by the Master at Arms. Particular care should be taken that the Master at Arms or Outer Guard do not converse in a frivolous manner with the candidate while he is being prepared, but on the contrary a grave solemnity should mark the whole transaction.

Master at Arms (gives one rap); Inner Guard (1 rap); Master at Arms (2 raps); Inner Guard (2 raps) Master at Arms (3 raps); Inner Guard (3 raps).

Inner Guard.—"Who comes here, and what do you desire?"

Master at Arms.—"The Master at Arms of this Lodge, with a stranger who desires to become a Retainer of, and asks to be initiated into the mysteries of the First or Initiatory Rank of Page of this Chivalric Order."

Inner Guard.—"Chancellor Commander, a stranger knocks for admission to these portals who desires to become a Retainer of, and asks to be initiated into the mysteries of the First or Initiatory Rank of Page of this Chivalric Order."

Chancellor Commander.—"It is my order, as Chancellor Commander, that you admit him without further challenge."

(Inner Guard opens door.")

The Master at Arms enters with the candidate and conducts him around the room very slowly three times, (during which time the utmost silence must prevail, with the exception of the music, which should be of a solemn character,) and then halts before the chair of the Chancellor Commander.

Master at Arms.—"Chancellor Commander, a stranger stands before you, who desires to become a Retainer of, and asks to be initiated into the mysteries of the First or Initiatory Rank of Page in this Chivalric Order."

Chancellor Commander (addressing the candidate.)—"Stranger, clad as you are, and devoid of the gift of sight, I ask you, as Chancellor Commander of this Lodge, is this your desire?"

Candidate answers.

Chancellor Commander.—"Before proceeding further with this ceremony, it is a duty incumbent upon me to propound to you several questions touching your qualifications to become a member of this Order in any Rank. I will therefore ask: Do you believe in the existence of a Supreme Being?"

Candidate answers.

Chancellor Commander.—"Are you of sound bodily health?"

Candidate answers.

Chancellor Commander.—"Have you ever before applied to become a member of the Order of Knights of Pythias?"

Candidate answers.

Chancellor Commander.—"Stranger, have you fully considered the weighty duties that will devolve upon you when once a member of this Order in any Rank that it may confer, or do you enter these portals from mere idle curiosity?"

Candidate answers.

Chancellor Commander.—"You are probably aware, and if not I will now inform you, that when you are duly become a member of, and progress in the Order of Knights of Pythias, that you are entitled to all the honors, benefits and privileges arising from the several Grades of Rank, as attained, that can in any way be bestowed upon you. Now, therefore, having given you these assurances on my part, as Chancellor Commander, and in all sincerity and kindness, I ask you in the name of the order universal, what are we to expect from you in return?"

Candidate answers.—**"Obedience."**

Chancellor Commander.—"Such being your pledge, I ask, Are you willing to take upon yourself a solemn and binding obligation to keep forever secret all that you may see or hear or hereafter be instructed in, of the mysteries of this Order—an obligation which we have all taken, and one which I, as Chancellor Commander, assure you will in no wise affect your religion or your politics?"

Candidate answers.

Chancellor Commander.—"Are you keenly sensible as to the solemnity, and willing to conform and live up to the requirements of, an obligation of this character?"

Candidate answers.

Chancellor Commander.—"Are you aware that, once you have taken upon yourself this solemn and binding obligation, there is no receding from its demands?"

Candidate answers.

Chancellor Commander.—"Should you waver in your purpose, there is yet time to withdraw." (Pause.) "Do you still desire to proceed?"

Candidate answers.

Chancellor Commander.—"The Master at Arms will conduct the stranger to the Prelate of this Lodge, who will administer to him the solemn and binding obligation of the First, or Initiatory Rank of Page, of this Chivalric Order."

Master at Arms conducts stranger round the lodge three times, or until everything is prepared for administering the obligation. Immediately upon leaving the station of the Chancellor Commander the attendants should, as noiselessly as possible, stand ready to turn down the lights very low, and to light the urns that are stationed at each end of the open coffin, containing a complete human skeleton. As soon as all is in readiness the Master at Arms brings the candidate opposite and in front of the Prelate.

Master at Arms.—"Prelate, by direction of the Chancellor Commander I present to you a stranger who desires to take upon

himself the solemn and binding obligation of the **First, or Initia-**
tory Rank of Page, he having so signified his desire and willingness to conform thereto."

Prelate (to candidate).—"Stranger is this your desire?"

Candidate answers.

Prelate.—"Master at Arms, why is the stranger brought before
me in this garb?"

Master at Arms.—"To indicate the purity of his intentions,
white being the emblem thereof."

Prelate.—"I most willingly and cheerfully accept the emblem,
indicating as it does, that purity of heart and rectitude of conduct which are essential to obtain admission into this, the First,
or Initiatory Rank and Grade of our Chivalric Order. Has the
stranger been instructed as to the serious, solemn and binding
obligation he is about to take upon himself?"

Master at Arms.—"He has."

Prelate.—"Stranger, is this so?" ·

Candidate answers.

. Prelate.—"Master at Arms, you will place the candidate in
proper position, by his kneeling upon both knees, his left hand
on the left breast, over his heart; his right hand extended, palm
down, and resting on the Book of Law and Swords of Defence."

The Master at Arms causes the candidate to kneel by the side
of the open **coffin** containing a human skeleton, the Prelate on
the opposite side, and places his right hand on the Holy Bible,
that rests on the (two) Swords of Defence which lie across the
coffin and rest on it, handles of swords towards the Prelate, crossed with points towards the candidate, and his left hand on the
left breast over his heart. The officers and members assembled
around the Prelate all kneel, the members covering him with
their lances, if so armed, until the candidate has assumed the obligation, when the lances are raised to a perpendicular position,
and remain so until he leaves the room. (See diagram.)

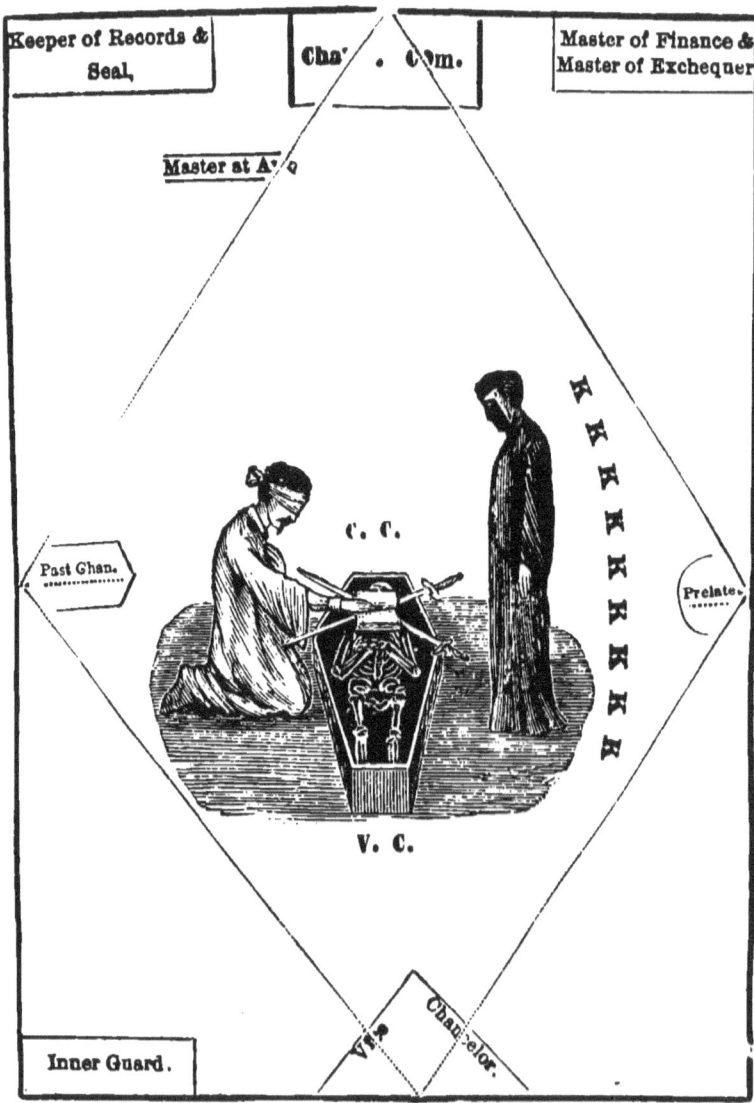

Keeper of Records & Seal,

Cha' . Com.

Master of Finance & Master of Exchequer

Master at A', Q

Past Chan.

C. C.

Prelate.

V. C.

Vice

Chancelor.

Inner Guard.

CANDIDATE TAKING OBLIGATION, FIRST, OR INITIATORY RANK.

The cut shows the Prelate administering the obligation. The Chancellor Commander is at the head of the coffin, the Vice Chancellor at the foot, the Past Chancellor at the right of the candidate, the Master at Arms at the left, the Prelate opposite the candidate as shown. On each side of the Prelate is a Knight and the rest of the Knights kneel in rows in a semicircle back of the Prelate.

Master at Arms.—"Prelate, the candidate is duly prepared."

Prelate.—"Stranger, as you are about to subscribe to an obligation of great solemnity, it is but just that you should be in rightful possession of all your mental faculties, and as by the rules of our order you have hitherto been deprived of sight, for reasons which must have been evident to you, the Master at Arms will now remove the bandage, that you may be able to see as well as to hear."

Master at Arms removes bandage. Prelate kneels opposite; the brethren kneeling in a half circle opposite and facing candidate, with lowered lances.

Prelate.—"You will now repeat after me:"

OBLIGATION FIRST RANK.

"I, (your name) in the presence of these true and tried brethren do most solemnly promise, declare and swear, that I will never reveal to the day of my death and will keep secret all the mysteries of which I have been, or may be hereafter instructed in; and that I will keep forever sacred within the deep recesses of my heart, even in the sanctuary thereof, veiled from all human eyes, all the passwords, grips, signs and countersigns, together with each and every secret that I may hereafter be instructed in; except it be in a regular Lodge, duly instituted and working under proper legal authority, of the Order of Knights of Pythias, or to an authorized officer, or duly qualified member of the Order, of proper rank; and to the latter only after strict and satisfactory examination, sufficient to warrant my conversing with him or them on or about the same.

"I further promise and declare, that I will ever and always relieve a distressed brother; that I will warn him of any danger which I may know to threaten him, and will fly to his succor and aid whenever and wherever I may be convinced by eye or ear that he is in need thereof.

"I further declare and say, that I am not now, nor will I ever so long as I remain a member of the Order of Knights of Pythias, become a member of, or affiliate with any body, under whatsoever name, claiming to be a higher, a branch, or side degree of the Knights of Pythias, unless under the control, guidance of and fully recognized as such by the Supreme Lodge Knights of Pythias of the World.

"I further promise and declare, that I will observe all the rules and regulations required by the Constitution and By-Laws of this or any other Lodge of this Order that I may become a member of, and to the best of my ability will live up to all the requirements of the Order.

"In evidence of which I herewith pledge my sacred word of honor. So help me God, and keep me steadfast in this my first and binding obligation in the Order of Knights of Pythias."

Prelate.—"In token of your sincerity you will now kiss the Book that is open before you, which is our Book of Law, and is the Holy Bible."

Candidate does so, and while peforming this act the following is chanted:

INITIATORY ANTHEM.

"Mid the deep hush that o'er the earth is creeping,
Father, I come to thee;
With humbleness of heart I kneel entreating—
Be merciful to me."

When through, the Prelate, Chancellor Commander, Vice Chancellor, Master at Arms and candidate all rise, (the rest remain kneeling), and while standing in their different positions, the Prelate says:

Prelate.—"Stranger, you have taken upon yourself an obligation of great solemnity. It is perhaps needless for me to enjoin upon you the great necessity of your living up to, in each and every particular, all the requirements therein contained. You have pledged your most solemn word of honor—all that man can pledge of inestimable worth. You have called upon the Supreme Ruler of the Universe to help you in keeping inviolate the trust confided to you. As a retainer, (for by that title I can now address you), I feel that you will keep sacred this obligation, and I have every reason to believe that you will become a faithful friend, a good companion and an exemplary Page. This obligation you have taken over the **Skeleton*** of our honored and revered patron saint, Pythias. This you can never forget. With

*The word here is optional with the Prelate. He may use either of the following words: Emblem, Symbol, or **Skeleton** .

pleasure I present you with a sprig of myrtle, emblematic of **Friendship**, which is the motto of this Rank. This you will retain carefully until you may be called upon to relinquish it. Finally, I would call your attention to the arrangement of the Book of Law and Swords of Defence in this Rank. (Explains them. See page 15.)

Prelate, (addressing Master at Arms).—"Master at Arms, you will now conduct the Retainer to the ante-room and prepare him to receive further and full instruction, that will entitle him to the Rank and Grade of Page."

All remain kneeling till they retire from the room. The lights are then turned up, the **Coffin** removed, flambeaus extinguished, etc. The Master at Arms prepares the candidate, by removing the **White Robe** and investing him with his coat and vest. He is then brought back to the door.

Master at Arms; one rap; two raps; three raps.

Inner Guard.—"Who comes here?"

Master at Arms.—"Retainer John Brown, who is desirous of receiving further knowledge of the mysteries and work of the First, or Initiatory Rank of Page in this Chivalric Order."

Inner Guard.—"Chancellor Commander, Retainer John Brown applies for further instruction in the work of the First, or Initiatory Rank of Page in this Chivalric Order."

Chancellor Commander.—"As Chancellor Commander of this Lodge, it is my order that you admit him without further challenge."

Inner Guard (opening the door).—"Master at Arms, it is the order of the Chancellor Commander that he be admitted without further challenge."

The Master at Arms enters with, and conducts the candidate twice around the Lodge, and halts before the Vice Chancellor.

Master at Arms.—"Vice Chancellor, I present you Retainer John Brown, for further instruction in the work of the First, or Initiatory Rank of Page in this Chivalric Order."

Vice Chancellor.—"Has he conformed to the Law and taken the obligation?"

Master at Arms.—"He has."

Vice Chancellor.—"How am I as Vice Chancellor, to be convinced that he has subscribed and will conform to the obligaion of this, the First, or Initiatory Rank of Page in this Chivalric Order?"

Master at Arms.—"He is in possession of the sprig of myrtle."

Vice Chancellor.—"To those of the First, or Initiatory Rank of Page in this Chivalric Order, what is the myrtle emblematic of?"

Master at Arms.—**"Friendship,** like unto that which bound Damon to Pythias."

Vice Chancellor.—"What does it teach?"

Master at Arms.—"Universal Fraternity and Benevolence, especially to those of the different grades of rank of our Chivalric Order, and to all worthy people, wherever existing."

Vice Chancellor.—"How does it instruct us?"

Master at Arms.—"It instructs us that, in the mind of a **Page** of this Order, those virtues should be as expansive as the azure arch of heaven, as binding as his obligation and pure as was that of our great prototypes, Damon and Pythias."

Vice Chancellor.—"Retainer John Brown I cheerfully accept the symbol as an earnest of your intentions, (takes it from him,) and will proceed to instruct you in the raps, secret signs, countersigns and passwords of this the First, or Initiatory Rank of Page, to which pay particular attention, as upon your knowledge of them will in part depend your future progress in this Order."

"Upon coming into the Lodge, you will knock at the outer door in any, or a usual manner. It will be opened by the Outer Guard, who will admit you to the ante room. After clothing yourself in the proper regalia, or insignia of this Rank, which is Blue, you will apply at the inner door, and give first one, then two, then three raps in this order, which will be answered in a like manner from within. You will then give your name and Rank, together with the name and number of your Lodge, and this password, **Friend** (whispers it in his ear,) which will admit you. You will then advance to the center of the room and salute the Chancellor Commander in this manner:

SIGN OF FRIENDSHIP OR COURTESY.

Form a link with the second finger of each hand, the back of the left hand up and the back of the right hand forward; the forearms forming the base of a triangle. [See cut.]

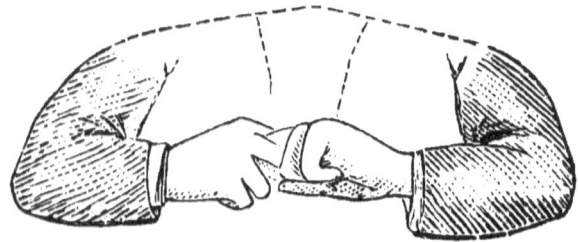

"This is called the sign of Friendship or Courtesy, and is always used on entering or retiring from the Lodge when open in the Rank of Page. It is recognized by the Chancellor Comder by giving the same sign or by a wave of the hand."

"There are three other signs, (in which, while instructing, you will please follow me.)"

THE SIGN OF RECOGNITION

Is given thus: Place your right thumb near the end of your two first fingers of same hand as though holding a pen to write, then smooth the hair back over the right ear with the two fingers, nails next to the head, three times, and is answered by the person saluted with the left hand in same manner.

The Sign of Caution, which is given in two ways, namely, audibly and inaudibly, is as follows:

INAUDIBLE SIGN OF CAUTION.

Raise right hand and with thumb and forefinger squeeze the wings of the nose. This is done three times, noiselessly, in quick succession drawing the hand six or eight inches from the nose after each squeeze.

AUDIBLE SIGN OF CAUTION.

Made in the same way as Inaudible Sign, but to attract attention give a quick snuff each time as thumb and finger are being withdrawn from the nose.

ANSWER.—Same as sign.

The Sign of Distress is given in this manner:

SIGN OF DISTRESS.

Strike the hands together three times, right hand uppermost.

There is a hailing word in connection with the Sign of Distress, which is **nomad**, (Damon backwards).

ANSWER.—**Damon**.

Vice Chancellor (addressing Master at Arms).—"The Master at Arms will now conduct the Page to our Chancellor Commander for final instruction."

Master at Arms.—"Chancellor Commander, under instruction of the Vice Chancellor, I present you Page John Brown for final instruction and examination in that Rank."

Chancellor Commander.—"Has the Page been taught the Signs and Passwords that will indicate his Rank as a Page?"

Master at Arms.—"He has been instructed therein by the Vice Chancellor."

Chancellor Commander.—"Page John Brown, as an evidence of the attention you have paid in what you have been instructed by the Vice Chancellor, you will be kind enough to give me the Sign of Friendship or Courtesy of this Rank?"

Candidate forms a link with second finger of each hand, forearms forming base of a triangle.

Chancellor Commander.—"How is it recognized by the Chair?"

Candidate.—"Chancellor Commander answers by same sign or by wave of his hand."

Chancellor Commander.—"The Sign of Recognition?"

Candidate quickly passes two first fingers of right hand, with ball of thumb near their end and nails next to head, back over right ear three times.

Chancellor Commander.—"Its answer?"

Candidate.—"Sign made with left hand in same manner."

Chancellor Commander.—"The Sign of Caution in both ways?"

Candidate.—"Thumb and forefinger drawn from nose three times, if for audible sign snuffing air, if for inaudible sign not doing so."

Chancellor Commander.—"Its answer?"

Candidate.—"The same."

Chancellor Commander.—"The Sign of Distress?"

Candidate.—"Strike hands together three times, right hand uppermost."

Chancellor Commander.—"In the absence of being able to use it, what do you do?"

Candidate.—"Use word Nomad, which is Damon backwards."

Chancellor Commander.—"What is the answer?"

Candidate.—"Damon."

Chancellor Commander.—"It now only remains for me to instruct you in the Grip and use of the Gavel or Truncheon of authority. The Grip is given in this manner."

GRIP, FIRST RANK.

Each extend the right hand, opening the fingers between the second and third as shown in upper cut, and grasp each other by the first two fingers, closing the other fingers as shown in lower cut.

Chancellor Commander.—"There is a word or cover key con·

nected with this grip which I will show you how to arrive at."

The Chancellor Commander and Master at Arms holding each other by the grip engage in the following colloquy :

Chancellor Commander.—"Say what is this?"

Master at Arms.—   "A good thing."

Chancellor Commander.—"Most people would say so."

Master at Arms.—   "Some would."

Chancellor Commander.—"O, would they?"

Master at Arms.—   "No doubt."

The first letters of each sentence spell the word **Samson**; the name of the grip, which means **Strength** as its name indicates."

Chancellor Commander.—"The Gavel is an instrument made use of to preserve order, call the Lodge to their feet and seat them. (One rap), one rap calls the Lodge to order, and in opening or closing calls up the officers addressed. (Two raps), two raps calls the Lodge to their feet. (Three raps), three raps seats the Lodge."

Chancellor Commander.—"Do you remember having heard these raps before, and if so, how and when are they used?"

Candidate answers and they are again explained to him by Chancellor Commander."

The knocks at the inner door to gain admission to the Lodge when open in the first rank: The brother wishing to gain admission gives (1) rap; Inner Guard (1) rap; brother (2) raps; Inner Guard (2); brother (3); Inner Guard (3). Inner Guard then opens the wicket and the brother whispers his name and the word **Friend** to the Inner Guard who closes the wicket and reports his name to the Chancellor Commander who directs that he be admitted. In case it is a visitor from some other Lodge he will give his own name, the name and number of his Lodge and the password **Friend**.

Chancellor Commander.—"You have now received all the instruction that can be given you in this, the First, or Initiatory Rank of Page. It will be necessary for you to become proficient in all the secret work, so that you can make yourself known to members as having received the First, or Initiatory Rank of Page of this order.

"In conclusion, I have a few words to say touching the motto of this degree: **Friendship** has for ages been looked upon as the corner stone of every secret society. For the purpose of practically testing the great principle of fellowship, numerous orders have been established over the entire globe. Our honored patron, the valiant knight from whom our order takes its name, gave a most heroic example of pure **Friendship**, that the whole world might follow. Confined, at his own request, in a loathsome dungeon, a hostage for Damon, that his friend might see his wife and child ere death snatched him from them forever; the cruel tyrant that had condemned the friend of Pythias to the block, gave him but six short hours to live. Damon's wife and child were leagues away. Mounted on a swift steed, he flew to them; and when he had given them the last fond embrace, he starts to return, and finds that his slave, to save his life, had slain his steed. The hour approaches, the dread moment has arrived, and Pythias is brought to the scaffold to suffer for his friend. Does he falter there? No! Does he murmur? No! but with his face all radiant with smiles, exclaims: ' 'Tis sweet to die for those we love.' At the last moment Damon arrives, and Pythias is saved. The would-be sacrifice was prevented by an all-wise Providence Let the teachings of that day remain fresh in the memory of all. The virtue, **Friendship**, should be emulated by us. We, as a society, are sworn to exercise it in our midst. Let us not forget its teachings, but rather keep the motto ever in view, that when we are called upon to enter the dark valley of the shadow of death, we can pass from this earthly sphere with malice towards none, and at peace with the whole world."

Chancellor Commander (addressing Master at Arms)—"Master at Arms, you will now face Page John Brown to the Lodge, and clothe him in the proper regalia of the First, or Initiatory Rank of a Page of this Order."

Master at Arms faces candidate towards Vice Chancellor's station, and invests him with the proper regalia.

Chancellor Commander (two raps).—"Officers and Brethren of the First, or Initiatory Rank of Page of this Chivalric Order, permit me to introduce to you Page John Brown, who has been regularly initiated, according to the established formulas and ceremonies, as a Page of this Order."

After the public introduction, the Chancellor Commander gives one rap and says:—"The Lodge will be at ease until the sound of the gavel at the Chancellor Commander's station."

REMARKS ON FIRST RANK.

"Man-like it is to fall into sin,
Fiend-like it is to dwell therein."

With charity we suppose that the great multitude of the Knights of Pythias are neither wilfully ignorant nor willing to remain guilty.

Will these members of the order, as well as others who read this revelation, carefully compare it with the "Book of Law, the Holy Bible," and if the two are antagonistic, withhold their sympathy and financial and moral support from the order of the Knights of Pythias, as an institution containing germs whose development will prove fatal to the privileges which they most highly prize.

The Knights have one excellent principle, if they mean what they say, viz: the adoption of the Holy Bible as their book of law.

Compare the practices of this order with the precepts of the Bible. "To the law and to the testimony; if they speak not according to this word it is because there is no light in them." Isaiah 8 : 20.

"If therefore the light that is in thee be darkness, how great is that darkness." Luke 6 : 23.

The lodge members in preparing to receive a candidate for initiation in the first rank array themselves in *Masks and Black Robes.* The Book of Law says, "provide things honest in the sight of all men." Romans 12 : 17.

Is not such a preparation contrary to the "simplicity and godly sincerity" in which Paul rejoiced ? 2 Cor. 1 : 12, and from which he feared Christians would be led away by Satan ? "But I fear, lest by any means, as the serpent beguiled Eve through his subtilty, so your minds should be corrupted from the simplicity that is in Christ." Sec. 2 Cor. 11 : 3.

These remarks apply with equal force to the manner in which the candidate is introduced.

His blindfolded eyes; his white robe; the raps at the lodge room door; the questions and answers following; the slow and solemn parade about the lodge room, all show that it is contrary to the honest yea, yea and nay, nay inculcated by God's word.

But the most fundamental and fatal feature of the order, stamping it an enemy of mankind, by ignoring Christ, may be found in embryo in this question asked in the early part of the initiation. "Do you believe in the existence of a Supreme Being ?"

"He that honoureth not the Son, honoureth not the Father which hath sent Him." John 5 : 23.

Thus early in their ritual the Knights favorably recognize a man-devised Deism, and ignore Christ who is "the power of God and the wisdom of God." 1 Cor. 1 : 24.

This order has a form of godliness but denies the power thereof. (see also prayers on opening and closing the lodge.) The Book of Law commands:—"*From such turn away.*" 2 Tim 3 : 5.

The friendship inculcated by this order will be noticed at the close of the *second* rank.

The obligations of the three ranks partake of one spirit and will be noticed at the close of the amplified **third rank.**

FORM OF PASSING FROM RANK OF PAGE TO THAT OF ESQUIRE.

The Lodge being at ease, the Chancellor Commander assumes his chair and gives one rap. Immediate observance must be given it. The officers repair to their chairs and members to their seats.

Chancellor Commander (one rap).—"Brother Master at Arms."

Master at Arms (rising promptly).—"Chancellor Commander."

Chancellor Commander.—"Are you satisfied, from your previous examinations, that all present are qualified to remain in this Lodge of the First, or Initiatory Rank of Page?"

The Master at Arms, it is supposed, will always bear in mind the fact that members admitted between the first and second sections of the work have not been examined by him."

Master at Arms (looking around.)—"I am so satisfied Chancellor Commander."

Chancellor Commander.—"Are you satisfied that all present are qualified to remain in the Second, or Armorial Rank of Esquire?"

Master at Arms.—"I am" (or am not—as the case may be,) "so satisfied."

Should the Master at Arms respond in the affirmative, the Chancellor Commander gives the rap, calling the Inner Guard up, and passes fully to the Second Rank.

Should the Master at Arms answer in the negative, he will prove those in doubt, if there are any besides the candidate or candidates just initiated, and says:

Master at Arms.—"Chancellor Commander."

Chancellor Commander.—"Brother Master at Arms."

Master at Arms.—"I find all qualified except the Page (or Pages) just initiated, or awaiting to be proved in the Rank of Esquire."

Chancellor Commander.—"Brother Master at Arms, you will invite those not qualified to remain in the Second or Armorial Rank of Esquire to approach the altar, salute the Chancellor Commander and retire."

While they are at the altar, and having made the sign, any announcement required will be made to them, when escorted by the Master at Arms to the inner door, they retire from the lodge room and the Master at Arms repairs to his station.

Chancellor Commander (one rap).—"Brother Inner Guard."

Inner Guard (rising promptly).—"Chancellor Commander."

Chancellor Commander.—"It is my order that —— Lodge, No. ——, Knights of Pythias, of the Grand Jurisdiction of ——, be now closed in the First, or Initiatory Rank of Page, and opened in that of the Second, or Armorial Rank of Esquire. This order you will communicate to the Brother Outer Guard, and bid him act in conformity therewith."

Inner Guard (goes out and says).—"Brother Outer Guard it is the order of the Chancellor Commander that this Lodge be closed in the First, or Initiatory Rank of Page, and opened in that of the Second, or Armorial Rank of Esquire; you will perform your duties in conformity therewith."

Outer Guard.—"The commands of the Chancellor Commander shall be obeyed."

Inner Guard (returning).—"Chancellor Commander."

Chancellor Commander.—"Brother Inner Guard."

Inner Guard.—"The Outer Guard has received your commands and will obey them."

Chancellor Commander.—"Therefore the officers and members will give strict attention that the Lodge is now open in the Second, or Armorial Rank of Esquire."

Chancellor Commander (two raps, all rise).—"Advance your shields by placing your left hand on the left breast."

All give that sign and while under it the Chancellor Commander says: "I am also satisfied in my triangle; Brother Vice Chancellor, are you satisfied in yours?"

Vice Chancellor.—"I am, Chancellor Commander."

Chancellor Commander.—"Recover!"

All drop the sign and assume a standing position, arms down."

Chancellor Commander.—"All is well. Brother Master at Arms you will arrange the Book of Law and Swords of Defence." (See page 15.)

After which Chancellor Commander gives three raps. (All seated.)

INITIATION.

The Page or Pages are taken to the ante-room in ordinary dress, and each one given a shield, which he is required to put on his left forearm, and from thence to the door of the Lodge, on the outside of which is suspended a shield, on which the Master at Arms gives **one** rap.''

Inner Guard (through the wicket).—"Who comes here! Who strikes upon the shield of this Lodge of the Second, or Armorial Rank of Esquire, in this Chivalric Order?"

Master at Arms.—"Page John Brown, who is desirous, if the officers and members will permit, of being further advanced in knowledge in this Chivalric Order, by being proved in the Second, or Armorial Rank of Esquire."

Inner Guard (closes wicket).—"Chancellor Commander, the Master at Arms presents Page John Brown, who asks· that he may be further advanced by being proved in the Second, or Armorial Rank of Esquire in this Chivalric Order."

Inner Guard opens the door a few inches, that the candidate may hear the following dialogue:

Chancellor Commander.—"If there are no objections, he will be admitted."

Vice Chancellor (promptly, in a loud tone). — "Chancellor Commander, before the Page is admitted, I would like to inquire of the Keeper of Records and Seal, if he has served a proper time in that rank, and is qualified to bear arms in this, the Second, or Armorial Rank of Esquire, in this Chivalric Order?"

Keeper of Records and Seal.—"He has."

Prelate (promptly, in a loud tone.—"Chancellor Commander, has the Page shown by his strict fidelity to the Order that he is entitled to this, the Second, or Armorial Rank of Esquire, in this Chivalric Order?"

Chancellor Commander.—"To the best of my knowledge and belief, he has."

Master of Exchequer (promptly, in a loud tone.)—"Chancellor Commander, is the Page's reputation among the members of this

Chivalric Order and his fellow men, such as should commend him to the Lodge as a proper person to receive the Second, or Armorial Rank of Esquire?"

Chancellor Commander.—"He has conformed to the law of the First, or Initiatory Rank of Page, and I see no reason why he should not be admitted to full fellowship with the Esquires of this Chivalric Order. No legal objection having been advanced it is my order, as Chancellor Commander, that the Page be admitted under the usual formulas."

Inner Guard (opens door).—"Master at Arms, there being no legal objection advanced, the Chancellor Commander orders that the Page be admitted."

Master at Arms enters with the candidate, conducts him twice around the room, and halts before the chair of the Vice Chancellor.

Master at Arms.—"Vice Chancellor, I have the pleasure of presenting to you Page John Brown, who has received that rank in this Lodge, and having served a proper time as such, is desirous of being further advanced in the mysteries of this Chivalric Order, by being proved in the Second, or Armorial Rank of Esquire,"

Vice Chancellor.—"Page John Brown it is with unfeigned pleasure that I greet you as an aspirant for the honors of the Esquire's Rank, heartily congratulating you on the progress you have made, and of being thought worthy to be entitled thereto. It becomes my duty before proceeding further, to interrogate you as to whether you are willing to take upon yourself a binding obligation to keep forever secret the mysteries of the Second, or Armorial Rank in this Chivalric Order?"

Candidate answers.

Vice Chancellor.—"Master at Arms, you will conduct the Page to our Prelate, who will administer the obligation of the Second, or Armorial Rank of Esquire in the Order of Knights of Pythias."

The Master at Arms presents candidate before the Prelate at the altar, opposite to and facing him.

Master at Arms.—"Prelate, by direction of our Vice Chancellor, I present you Page John Brown, who is desirous of being further advanced in the mysteries of this Chivalric Order, for the purpose of taking upon himself the obligation of the Second, or Armorial Rank of Esquire."

Prelate.—"Page John Brown, is this your desire?"

Candidate answers.

The Prelate rising from his chair goes to the altar, which is turned so as to bring the sword handles towards the Prelate's station and points toward the candidate, and says: "You will advance your shield by placing your left hand on the left breast, over your heart; the left foot thrown forward, raise your right hand perpendicularly, with the hand clinched, as if in the act of striking a downward blow; in which position you will repeat after me:

Chancellor Commander, (two raps).

OBLIGATION, SECOND OR ARMORIAL RANK OF ESQUIRE.

"I, John Brown, in the presence of the true and tried Esquires here assembled, covered by my shield, and of my own free will and accord, do pledge my word and most sacred honor, that under any and every circumstance or position in which I may be placed, I will keep inviolate all the signs, passwords, grips or tokens of this the Esquire Rank of the Knights of Pythias, except it be when given in instruction in course of duty as, or to a properly authorized officer of a regular Lodge of this rank, or deputized authority as an examining committee to demand the same.

"And I specially promise that I will not write or indite upon anything movable or immovable, any of the private work of the Rank of Esquire, by which the secrets may become known, or suffer it to be done by another, if in my power to prevent; and that I will at all times and under all circumstances, aid and assist an Esquire in distress; that I will warn, counsel or shield him from any danger which I may know to threaten him or any member of his family. All this I promise and declare without mental reservation. So help me God, and keep me steadfast in this my second obligation of the Knights of Pythias."

Prelate.—"In token of your sincerity, you will now kiss the book that is open before you, which is our Book of Law, and is the Holy Bible."

Chancellor Commander (three raps).

Prelate.—"Esquire you have now taken upon yourself the solemn and binding obligation of the Second, or Armorial Rank of Esquire. It now remains for you to regulate your acts that those of this rank may say of you: "He is indeed truly an Esquire," remembering always that your Shield of Honor must be kept so bright in its purity of polish, that he who would say aught against its purity of purpose and act, would be rendered blind by its bright surface reflecting the dazzling sheen of your injured honor."

"Asking your special attention to the arrangement of the altar, Book of Law and Swords of Defence, which you will find highly important hereafter," (explains them); "the Master at Arms will now conduct you to the Chancellor Commander, who will instruct you in the signs, countersigns, grip and password, of this the Second, or Armorial Rank of Esquire in this Chivalric Order."

Master at Arms presents candidate before the Chancellor Commander."

Master at Arms.—"Chancellor Commander, by direction of the Prelate, I present you Esquire John Brown, for instruction in the secret work of this the Second, Armorial or Esquire's Rank in this Chivalric Order, he having taken the obligation in regular form, under his shield, and is thereby entitled to receive the same."

Chancellor Commander.—"Esquire, it now remains for me to instruct you, that you will be able to make yourself known to members as having attained the Second, or Armorial Rank of Esquire in this Chivalric Order, and also to prepare you, as of that rank, to take a seat in our midst."

"The numerical order of this Rank is that of the Second, or Armorial, wherein, as in olden times, you were permitted, for the first time, to carry a shield; the title of its members is Esquire, the motto is **Caution**, the color of the regalia or insignia, is yellow; the password is **Watch**; (pulls his watch from his pocket just before uttering the words); the sign of caution or courtesy, given on entering or retiring from the Lodge, when open in the Rank of Esquire, is;

SIGN OF CAUTION OR COURTESY, RANK OF ESQUIRE.

Place the right elbow in left hand and gently clinch the chin with the right hand. [See cut.]

COUNTERSIGN IN ANSWER: Same, or a wave of the hand by the Chancellor Commander.

THE ALARM: One rap.

SHIELD SIGN.

Raise right hand perpendicularly, with the hand clinched as if in the act of striking a downward blow, left hand over heart. Same position as when taking the obligation of this rank. [See cut.]

GRIP, RANK OF ESQUIRE.

Grasp left hands in ordinary way. No shake.

Chancellor Commander.—"Master at Arms, you will now retire with the Esquire to the ante-room, clothe him in the proper regalia of the Second or Armorial Rank of Esquire, in this Chivalric Order, and permit him to work his way into the Lodge without his shield."

Master at Arms and Esquire retire. Upon re-entering, after the candidate has given the sign, while at the Altar, the Chancellor Commander addresses him as follows·

Chancellor Commander.—"Esquire John Brown, before taking your seat, you will please come this way."

Candidate comes in front of station of Chancellor Commander.

Chancellor Commander.—"We have a Keeper of Records and Seal that is methodical in all his official business; he has given me a blank for you to fill out that he may know your hand-writing and the manner of spelling your name, the name and number of the street where you reside, etc." (hands him the blank.)

BLANK FOR CANDIDATE TO FILL OUT.

Name. . . . .

Residence. . . . .

Occupation. . . . .

Motto. . . . .

Password . . . .

Near the Chancellor Commander's station is a small writing desk so arranged that by touching a secret spring the top of the desk falls in and a bell is rung or a pistol fired and the word **Caution** in large letters appears.

When the candidate is handed the blank to fill out the desk is occupied by three of the brethren; one at each end and usually an officer in the center, whom we will suppose to be the Master of Exchequer. The Chancellor Commander calls out: "Brother Master of Exchequer you will please move from the desk, that the candidate may fill out the blank. (Master of Exchequer fails to hear, seems absorbed in his work.)

Chancellor Commander (louder.)—"Brother Master of Exchequer will you vacate that desk that the candidate may occupy it a moment?" (Still no attention is paid to the order.)

Chancellor Commander (still louder).—"Brother Master of Exchequer will you get up from that desk and go to your own station to do your writing?"

Master of Exchequer finally gathers up his writing materials and vacates the desk to the candidate. The brethren at each end keep up an earnest discussion on some subject and the Master at Arms stands behind the candidate, all of which is well designed to confuse him. When he begins to write the password the Master at Arms gives his shoulders a sudden jerk and the report of the pistol or ring of the bell with the tumbling of the desk and candidate to the floor creates a general confusion.

In some lodges the desk and the chair on which the candidate is seated tumble to pieces, and in a few lodges, as the spring is touched, two upright doors above the table suddenly open and a large pale hand about two feet long comes down on the candidate's hand.

Chancellor Commander (looking piously grave).—"Brother Master at Arms, what is the cause of this confusion?"

Master at Arms.—"The candidate has attempted to write the password."

The Chancellor Commander then delivers a short impromptu address to the candidate, something similar to the following:

Chancellor Commander (to candidate).—"I am astonished that a gentlemen of your general good appearance, and honest expression of countenance, having an established reputation for courteous conduct and unflinching integrity would come here and take solemn obligations and especially promise that you would not write or indite upon anything movable or immovable any of the private work of the Rank of Esquire, should attempt to violate your obligation even before the ceremony of conferring the Second Rank upon you is concluded."

Chancellor Commander.—"Brother Master at Arms you will divest the candidate of his regalia."

A brother rising says.—"I move that the candidate be suspended for 99 years."

The motion is seconded and stated to the Lodge by the Chancellor Commander, when after arguments *pro* and *con* the Chancellor Commander gives the candidate an opportunity to rise and explain, if he has any explanation to offer for the violation of his obligation.

After a humble apology by the candidate the motion for his suspension is withdrawn by the mover with consent of the second.

Should the candidate remember his obligation and not write the password he is complimented by the Chancellor Commander and is frequently shown what would have happened had he violated his word.

ADDRESS TO CANDIDATE, BY CHANCELLOR COM-
MANDER.

"Esquire John Brown, I assure you that this has not been done to trifle with your feelings, but to practically test the motto of the Second, or Armorial Rank of Esquire in this order. **Caution** has been defined as prudence, care, wariness and watchfulness; prudence not only in the lodges, but in your every day life; care in the proper transaction of your business; wariness in your every avocation, and a proper watchfulness of your family, that they may be permitted to enjoy every earthly blessing that is in your power to bestow upon them. The lesson that you have received is one that is likely to make a lasting and durable impression on your mind, and ever bring to your remembrance the solemn and binding obligation you have taken upon yourself never to reveal any of the secrets contained in this Rank of our Order. In the primary portion of these ceremonies, another practical exempli-fication of the teachings of this Rank was given you; and it was intended that all that was then said should reach your ears and furnish food for thought. To that end the Master at Arms brought you to the very threshhold of the Lodge, and the Inner Guard left the door ajar, as you no doubt thought accidentally. The Vice Chancellor questioned the Keeper of Records and Seal as to whether you had served a proper time as Page, it being im-peratively necessary, according to our rules, that the space of (one week, or two weeks as may be fixed by the By-laws. Usually one week) should elapse between the conferring of the different Grades of Rank in the Order. The Prelate questioned as to your fidelity to the order, and the Master of Exchequer interrogated as to your personal character, as no one whose reputation does not stand clear with the outer world can be received in friend-ship here. Therefore you perceive that **Caution** was used to its fullest extent before you were admitted to the Lodge. I feel sat isfied from the teachings that have been inculcated here, that you will prove yourself prudent and watchful, exhibiting the proper forethought in all your dealings, that is essential to your position in the world and proper station in this Order.

"Master at Arms, you will now face Esquire John Brown to the Lodge, (and if not having remembered his obligation, **and therefore** been divested of his regalia, the Chancellor **Commander** will continue) and clothe him in the proper regalia of the Second or Armorial Rank of an Esquire of this Order."

Master at Arms faces the candidate toward the Vice Chancellor's station, and invests him with the proper regalia.

Chancellor Commander (two raps).—"Officers and members of the Second, or Armorial Rank of this Chivalric Order, permit me to introduce to you Esquire John Brown, who has been regularly proved, according to the established formulas and ceremonies, as an Esquire of this Order."

After the public introduction the Chancellor Commander gives one rap and says:

"The Lodge will be at ease until the sound of the gavel at the Chancellor Commander's station."

REMARKS ON SECOND RANK.

Towards the close of the first rank the Chancellor Commander remarks: Friendship has for ages been looked upon as the Corner Stone of every Secret Society.

The editor of the *Peoria Transcript*, a shrewd business man, said of Masonry: "It is organized selfishness." Such we believe to be the opinion of this order, not only of honest persons outside of the Knights of Pythias but also of its own members.

What a narrow friendship is that which restricts its professed benefits to a favored few!

Not only are all women excluded from the order but at the session of the "Supreme Lodge of the World" at Richmond, Va., commencing March 9th, 1869 the application for a charter by a body of colored citizens of Philadelphia, "praying that they might be permitted to have and enjoy the great privileges and benefits of the Knights of Pythias," was refused."

"Thou shalt love thy neighbor as thyself." Matt 22; 39; is the rule of the Holy Scriptures. Christ gave His best and greatest blessings to "whosoever" would receive them. Like His heart all hearts should burn with a tender friendship for every member of the human family, and as we "have opportunity" we should, like the good Samaritan, help the needy wherever found.

Knights of Pythias offer their friendship to a select few. It is a spurious imitation of true friendship more fatal to the best interests of mankind than counterfeit money is to the interests of honorable commercial transactions.

The signs and grips which a candidate receives at the close of his obligation (and which he must conceal even from those nearest and dearest to him, if not members of the order) are put by the Bible into very bad company.

"A naughty person, a wicked man walketh with a froward mouth.

He winketh with his eyes, he speaketh with his feet, he teacheth with his fingers.

Frowardness is in his heart, he deviseth mischief continually; he soweth discord." Prov. 6: 12-14.

Life is too short, too solemn to be spent in counterfeiting anything valuable. Let us turn to Christ and with the grace which he gives to those who ask, exemplify by our own lives, and strengthen in every human being that we can influence, *Christian or Bible* friendship.

"Caution" is unquestionably needful and wise and were it properly exercised the Knights of Pythias and other secret orders would find a far smaller number who would submit to their wretched mummeries and tricks.

But who can fail to see that not a wise caution but suspicion and distrust is really what is taught by the low mean trick of a systematic effort of a body of men to confuse another, and having succeeded in doing so to jerk him from his chair to the floor, blow the desk at which he is seated in pieces and then reproach him with violating his obligation and vote to suspend him perpetually from membership. Could they possibly take a better method to convince the initiate that their pretended friendship is a sham and he must be on a sharp lookout for other tricks?

FORM OF PASSING FROM RANK OF ESQUIRE TO THAT OF KNIGHT.

The Lodge being at ease the Chancellor Commander resumes his chair and gives one rap. The officers repair at once to their chairs and members to their seats.

Chancellor Commander (one rap).—"Brother Master at Arms."

Master at Arms (rising).—"Chancellor Commander."

Chancellor Commander.—"Are you satisfied, from your previous examinations, that all present are qualified to remain in this Lodge of the Second, or Armorial Rank of Esquire?"

(The Master at Arms, it is supposed, will always bear in mind the fact that members admitted between the first and second sections of the work have not been examined by him.)

Master at Arms (looking around).—"I am so satisfied, Chancellor Commander."

Chancellor Commander.—"Are you satisfied that all present are qualified to remain in the Third, or Chivalric Rank of Knight?"

Master at Arms.—"I am (or am not—as the case may be) so satisfied."

Should the Master at Arms respond in the affirmative, the Chancellor Commander gives one rap, calling the Inner Guard up, and passes fully to the Third Rank.

Should the Master at Arms answer in the negative, he will prove those in doubt, if there are any besides the candidate or candidates just proved.

Master at Arms.—"Chancellor Commander."

Chancellor Commander.—"Brother Master at Arms."

Master at Arms.—"I find all qualified, except the Esquire (or Esquires) just proved or awaiting to be charged in the Rank of Knight."

Chancellor Commander.—"Brother Master at Arms, you will invite those not qualified to remain in the Third, or Chivalric Rank of Knight, to approach the Altar, salute the Chancellor Commander and retire."

While they are at the Altar, and having made the sign, any announcement required will be made to them, when escorted by the Master at Arms to the inner door, they retire from the lodge-room and the Master at Arms repairs to his station.

Chancellor Commander (one rap).—"Brother Inner Guard."

Inner Guard (rising.)—"Chancellor Commander."

Chancellor Commander.—"It is my order that ——— Lodge, No. —— Knights of Pythias, of the Grand Jurisdiction of ——, be now closed in the Second, or Armorial Rank of Esquire and opened in that of the Third, or Chivalric Rank of Knight. This order you will communicate to the Brother Outer Guard and bid him act in conformity therewith."

Inner Guard (going into ante-room) —"Brother Outer Guard, it is the order of the Chancellor Commander that the Lodge be closed in the Second, or Armorial Rank of Esquire and opened in that of the Third, or Chivalric Rank of Knight; you will perform your duties in conformity therewith."

Outer Guard.—"The commands of the Chancellor Commander shall be obeyed."

Inner Guard (returns).—"Chancellor Commander."

Chancellor Commander.—"Brother Inner Guard."

Inner Guard.—"The Outer Guard has received your commands, and will obey them."

Chancellor Commander.—"Therefore the officers and members will give strict attention that the Lodge is now open in the Third or Chivalric Rank of Knight."

Chancellor Com. (two raps, all rise).—"Advance your shields!"

ADVANCE YOUR SHIELDS.

Advance your shields, left hand clinched and held height of chin and a foot in front of it, back of hand from you.

Chancellor Commander.—"Parry!"

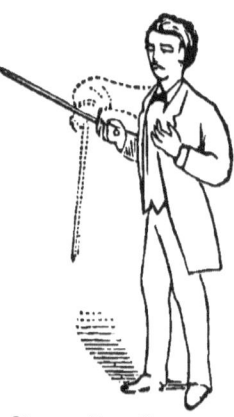

PARRY SIGN.

Bring sword to a "Present" and swing point from right to left as if to parry or ward off a blow. When sign is completed the right hand will be about a foot from the body and the sword will point about two feet in front of left foot.

Chancellor Commander (swords still held at "parry").—I am also satisfied in my triangle; Brother Vice Chancellor are you satisfied in yours?"

Vice Chancellor.—"I am, Chancellor Commander."

Chancellor Commander.—"Recover!" (All resume the ordinary position, arms down.)

Chancellor Commander.—"All is well." Brother Master at Arms you will arrange the Book of Law and Swords of Defence. (See page 15.)

This being done and the Master at Arms having returned to his station, the Chancellor Commander gives three raps. (All seated.)

INITIATION.

THIRD, OR CHIVALRIC RANK OF KNIGHT.

The Esquire is taken to the ante-room where he is instructed by the Master at Arms to say, in answer to any direct interrogatory made of him, "By what right does he make this demand?" the answer will be, "By that of being a brave man," or else get the candidate to authorize him—the Master at Arms—to do so for him, after which he is blindfolded, the shield put on his left forearm as in the preceding Rank; he is then conducted to the inner door, upon which there is no shield; the Master at Arms gives two raps, which are answered in the same manner from within, and the wicket is opened.

Inner Guard.—"Who comes here? Who dares to interrupt the proceedings of this Lodge while working in the Third, or Chivalric Rank of Knight?"

Master at Arms.—"Esquire John Brown, who having received the First, or Initiatory Rank of Page, been proved in the Second or Armorial Rank of Esquire, and passing a fair ballot, now declares himself a **Brave** man, and as such demands admittance to this Lodge of the Third, or Chivalric Rank of Knight."

Inner Guard (closes wicket.)—"Chancellor Commander, there is without an Esquire who has received the First or Initiatory Rank of Page, been proved in the Second or Armorial Rank of Esquire, and now demands admittance to this Lodge of the Third or Chivalric Rank of Knight."

Chancellor Commander.—"By what right does he make this demand?"

Inner Guard.—"By reason of having been initiated, proved, passing a fair ballot, and boasting himself a **Brave** man."

Chancellor Commander.—"Such being his pledge and demand and having attained the necessary preparatory Rank, it is my order as Chancellor Commander that you let him enter without further challenge."

The Master at Arms conducts the Esquire around the Castle Hall once and halts before the chair of the Chancellor Commander.

Master at Arms.—"Chancellor Commander, Esquire John Brown, who has been duly initiated as a Page, and proved as an Esquire, in this Chivalric Order, desires to receive the highest Rank conferred by this Lodge, by being instructed in the mysteries and passing through the ordeal that all brave Knights have done who have reached this summit of Pythian honors."

Chancellor Commander.—"Esquire, is this your demand?"

Candidate answers.

Chancellor Commander.—"Upon entering this Castle Hall as a Retainer, seeking the First or Initiatory Rank of Page, a requirement was exacted from and of you; do you remember what it was, and if so, will you state its nature?"

Candidate.—**Obedience.**"

Chancellor Commander.—"Brethren of the Knight's Rank, are you satisfied that the Esquire remembers and fully appreciates this requirement sufficient to advance him in our highest honors?"

(All.)—"We are."

Chancellor Commander.—"Upon attaining the First or Initiatory Rank of Page in this order, you were taught one great lesson. Do you remember what it was, and if so will you be kind enough to state the same?"

Candidate.—**"Friendship."**

Chancellor Commander.—"Brethren of the Knight's Rank, has the Esquire who demands advancement in our order merited as well as received your **Friendship.**"

(All.)—"He has."

Chancellor Commander.—"Upon reaching and being proved in the Second or Armorial Rank of Esquire of this order, you were taught another great lesson. Will you state what it was?"

Candidate.—**"Caution."**

Chancellor Commander.—"Brethren of the Knight's Rank, has the Esquire who stands before you as a candidate for the Third or Chivalric Rank of Knight, proven himself, to the best of your knowledge and belief, obedient, prudent, cautious and watchful?"

(All.)—"He has."

Chancellor Commander.—"This being so, Esquire, I can see no just reason why you should not be permitted to proceed in this Chivalric Order; but it is my duty to inform you that your cour-

age and confidence may be put to a severe test during the cere
monies through which you are about to pass, but should such be
the will of those around you assembled, and if, as you declare in
your demand, you are a **Brave** man, and will implicitly obey all
the orders given you, and requirements exacted during its progress, no accident can possibly befall you. On the contrary, if
you are not a man of iron nerve, or if you have made this demand from an unworthy motive, I tell you plainly and sincerely
that I cannot be answerable for any **injury** you may receive. To
assure you, however, that this Lodge, its officers and members
fully appreciate your position, I will, as Chancellor Commander,
state that the ordeal you may have to undergo is one, not only
dangerous in character, but of a fearful nature. (Sometimes the
Chancellor Commander requests the Keeper of Records and Seal
to read or quote the by-law of the Lodge, promising $10 per week
to a brother in case of disability and $100 for funeral expenses in
case of death and generally exaggerates the amount of the prom-
ised benefit.) Should your vaunted bravery fail you at the
crowning point of its consummation, by it we as an order prove
and exemplify the fact as to whether you have been truthful in
your former protestations of Friendship, such as was exhibited
by Damon towards Pythias, or the Caution, though unwise, as
shown by Lucullus in slaying his master's horse to preserve his
.life.

"Heretofore you have answered readily and promptly the interrogatories as made in the former and preceding grades of rank,
but the answers now to be given are of too serious a nature to be
lightly made, and I would therefore ask your greatest consideration before so doing; but to give you a last opportunity to elect
for yourself, I will state that it is not too late, if you so desire, to
be escorted hence and permitted to retire, (pause). With the
official assurance from me that no accident can befall an obedient
and friendly person, who is not only cautious but a truly brave
man, aspiring to the high rank of Knight, I ask, as Chancellor
Commander, in the name of this Lodge, its officers and members
around you assembled, do you still persist in your demand?"

Candidate answers.

Chancellor Commander.—"Are you willing to take upon your
self a solemn and binding obligation to keep forever secret the
mysteries of this Chivalric Rank of Knight?"

Candidate answers.

Chancellor Commander.—"Master at Arms, you will conduct the Esquire to our Prelate, who will administer the obligation of the Third and Chivalric Rank of Knighthood in this Order."

Master at Arms presents candidate before the Prelate at the Altar, opposite to and facing him.

Master at Arms.—"Prelate, by order of the Chancellor Commander of this Lodge, I present Esquire John Brown, who having been initiated as a Page and proved in the Second or Armorial Rank of Esquire, now declares himself a **Brave** man, and as such demands that he be obligated in the Third or Chivalric Rank of Knight in this Order."

Prelate.—"Esquire John Brown, do you declare yourself a **Brave** man, and make this demand of your own volition?"

Candidate answers.

Prelate.—"Master at Arms, why is he thus blindfolded?"

Master at Arms.—"That he might be conducted through this Castle Hall without being able to discover any of the secrets or ceremonies of the Knight Rank of our Order, should he fail to insist in his demands before the Chancellor Commander."

Prelate.—"Since the Esquire insists in his demands, you will remove the hoodwink, (which being done, the Prelate continues,) and place him in proper position, at the Altar, to take the obligation, by advancing his shield in placing his left hand on his left breast, over the heart, advancing his right foot, his right hand resting on the Book of Law and grasping the hilt of the Sword of Defence before him as if making a parry with the sword, in which position he will assume the obligation."

Master at Arms places candidate in proper position.

Chancellor Commander.—(Two raps.)

OBLIGATION RANK OF KNIGHT.

Prelate, rising, goes to the Altar and says:

"(You will now repeat after me.) I, (your name) do most solemnly and sincerely promise and declare, under the penalties of my former obligations, that I will never reveal, directly or indirectly, any of the signs, tokens or mysteries of this Rank of **Bravery**, or those of any other Rank of the Knights of Pythias, to any person not properly authorized by this, or a Lodge working under the control of a regularly constituted Grand Lodge, recognized by the Supreme Lodge Knights of Pythias of the

World, to receive the same; except it be a just and lawful Knight, whom I shall know to be legally entitled to receive the same, or within the Castle Hall of a just and regularly constituted Lodge, subordinate to the Supreme Lodge, Knights of Pythias of the World.

"I further promise and declare, never to communicate, by word, syllable, letter, sign or character, the semi-annual password to any person, save and except the proper officers within a Lodge, or in course of duty, acting in capacity of Chancellor Commander, Grand Chancellor or his deputy, or Supreme Chancellor or his deputy.

"I further promise to obey all orders that may be given me, emanating from the Supreme, Grand, this or any other Lodge of this Order of which I may become a member, or any competent authority issuing the same, so long as they do not conflict with my political or religious liberty. And if I ever, by word or sign, expose the secret work or ceremonies of this Order, in an unauthorized manner, or fail in any of my obligations, may I suffer all the anguish and torments possible for man to suffer. All this I promise and declare, without any mental reservation whatever. So help me God, and keep me steadfast."

"Prelate.—"Esquire John Brown, in testimony of your sincerity, you will now kiss the Book that is open before you, which is our Book of Law, the Holy Bible." (Kisses the book.)

Chancellor Commander.—(Three raps.)

Prelate.—"Esquire, you have now taken the obligation that ties you to us, and I hail you as an aspirant to the honors due to a Knight of this Order. You must ever remember your obligation, and the purpose of your shield in the Second or Armorial Rank of Esquire in this Order. You have seen how easily you might have fallen into an error, but for the interposition of a brother. Let the solemnity of that occurrence be ever present in your mind and emblazoned upon your shield and memory, to stimulate you to fulfill and keep inviolate every obligation taken by you. The obligation to which you have just subscribed, imposes a condition to obey all orders which may be given you, so long as they do not conflict with your civil or religious liberty. You have also stated in this Lodge that you are a man of courage. That assertion remains yet to be proven; and for the last time inviting your attention to the arrangement of the **Altar,** Book of Law and Swords of Defence, (See page **15;**) I now consign you to our Master at Arms, who will proceed with you to the ante-room, properly equip and present you to the Chancellor Commander, before whom your bravery may be put to a severe test. Have confidence, should such be the case, and all will be well."

Master at Arms takes him out and equips him in the helmet, shield, baldric, belt and sword with no blade to its handle, but is firmly soldered to the scabbard. When thus equipped he knocks, is admitted and taken before the Chancellor Commander.

Master at Arms.—"Chancellor Commander, under the instructions of the Prelate, I present Esquire John Brown who has taken the obligation of the Chivalric Rank of Knight, in this Order, and now demands his final instructions."

Vice Chancellor.—"Chancellor Commander, before you proceed any further, I demand to know by what right he wears the uniform, equipments and arms of a Knight without having gone through an ordeal to test his claims to so high a rank in this Chivalric Order? I demand the ordeal!"

Chancellor Commander.—"I had hoped the Esquire's conduct had been such as to warrant the Lodge in waiving this fearful ceremonial; yet it is for the Lodge, in its sovereign capacity, to say. Brethren what say you, is it ordeal, or no ordeal?"

All.—"Ordeal, the ordeal!"

Chancellor Commander.—"The Lodge so decides. Master at Arms, you will repair to the armory of this Castle Hall, and bring forth the first implement of torture contained therein that your hand may fall upon, and produce it here—remember that it is my order that you select from all that are there in the dark."

Master at Arms retires, and things are heard to fall down, making noise, etc.; in the meantime the Chancellor Commander instructs an assistant to relieve the candidate of helmet, shield, etc., and the Master at Arms returns with his selection and places it before the candidate; the Chancellor Commander exhibits the "Property of the Third Rank," an oak plank with about thirty-six spikes set therein, and causes candidate to examine it closely, after which it is placed in position. The ceremonies are varied, the language extempore and is such as the Chancellor Commander thinks will make a deep impression on the candidate. Though the Chancellor Commander plainly intimates that there are a number of implements of torture, there is in fact only an oak plank about twenty inches square and two inches thick, filled with spikes of iron or steel, five or six inches long, called the "property"and another an exact imitation of the first in appearance, in which the teeth are rubber. In some cases blood is sprinkled on and between the spikes to make the effect the more terrifying to the mind of the candidate. The "property" being in position the Master at Arms conducts the candidate to a chair or the three steps facing the "property" and directs him to take off his boots, when the Chancellor Commander says: "Brother Master at Arms you will conduct the candidate this way."

He is conducted near the Chancellor Commander who then addresses him in a short impromptu speech in which he pictures the various tests and tortures suffered by others in past ages, thus still further exciting his feelings, while at the same time divert-ing his attention while the plank with rubber spikes in is put in place of the other.

He is then escorted by the Master at Arms and executioners to a chair two or three feet back of the "property" which is between the chair and the Chancellor Commander. He steps into the chair, faces the Chancellor Commander, and the Knights form in two rows about six feet apart facing inward, each wearing a mask and long black robe, the robes of the executioners extend-ing over the head with small holes to see through. When thus ready the Master at Arms says: "Chancellor Commander, the candidate is in proper position."

Chancellor Commander to candidate (moving forward and bringing his sword to a "carry").—"We are now going to test your protestations of friendship and your fidelity to your obli-gation. You have sworn you would obey all orders emenating from the Supreme Chancellor, Grand Chancellor or the Chancel-lor Commander of this Lodge. I now as Chancellor Commander of this Lodge order you to jump with both feet on those points."

If he does not promptly obey the Knights all say: "He hesi-tates, he hesitates," etc.

If he does not obey the second order to jump they cry: "Cow ard," etc.

If he does not obey the third order to jump the Chancellor Commander orders the executioners to put him on the points which they proceed to do, always bringing down both feet on the mock spikes and sometimes laying him down on them.

Should there be two candidates, after the first is tested he may be laid down with a white robe over him and red cloths at his feet, and when the second candidate comes to the test the first lies groaning as if in great agony. [This groaning humbug is not always practiced.] About one man in ten will jump under the impression that the board with spikes will be jerked away by some one.

[The above is extempore and other appropriate words may be used.].

When the foregoing or similar ceremonies are completed the Master at Arms conducts the candidate to the Vice Chancellor.

Master at Arms.—"Vice Chancellor, I present Esquire John Brown, who has passed the ordeal that all Knights of this order must undergo, and having so done, new demands from you the sign, countersign, password and grip of this the Third or Chivalric Rank of Knight, he being entitled thereto."

Vice Chancellor. - "My brother, as a **Brave** man, I (if he did not obey—cannot) greet you. May the lesson you have received to-night be impressed indelibly upon your mind. We find many obstructions laying in our path through life, which, to the timid may seem dangerous and deadly: but the truly courageous man may brave them all and find them mere shadows. And now, with the hope that you will ever show yourself as brave as (or if not obeying—a braver man than) you have during the progress of this ceremonial, I will, with pleasure, instruct you in the signs, countersigns, password and grip.

The sign of Bravery or Courtesy in the Rank of Knight is as follows:

SIGN OF BRAVERY OR COURTESY, THIRD RANK.

Form a triangle with forearms extending horizontally from you, points of fingers and thumbs together and spread out; heel of hands about five inches apart. (See cut.) This is called the visor sign.

VISOR SIGN ON ENTERING LODGE.

On entering to salute the Chancellor Commander, raise visor so as to touch the breast with the forefingers, the thumbs pointing downward Hands are then separated and with a gentle wave are brought to the side.

VISOR SIGN ON RETIRING FROM LODGE.

On retiring approach the Altar, face the Chancellor Commander and turn the visor (hands) down, so that the thumbs point up and the fingers down and then bring hands to side with a gentle wave.

The Countersign, given by the Chancellor Commander, is same as sign or a wave of the hand. The Password, given at the inner door, is **Confidence**. The Alarm at the inner door is two raps. The Grip is given in this manner:

GRIP, THIRD RANK.

Take each other by the right hand as for ordinary hand shake. When withdrawing hands press each other's forefinger with thumb and forefinger, gently, the whole length of finger, slightly crooking the ends of the forefingers and hooking or pressing them together at the points.

Vice Chancellor.—"Master at Arms, you will now conduct our newly tried and instructed brother to the Chancellor Commander for final examination, instruction and enrollment on the roster of this Lodge, as having that Rank. (He does so.)

Master at Arms.—"Chancellor Commander, by direction of the Vice Chancellor of this Lodge, I present to you Brother John Brown, who has been instructed in the sign, countersign, password and grip of the Third or Chivalric Rank of Knight, for final examination, instruction and enrollment on the roster of this Lodge as having that Rank."

Chancellor Commander.—"Brother John Brown, as an evidence of the attention paid to the instruction already given you, you will be kind enough to satisfy me that you are in possession of the sign.

Candidate gives the Visor Sign which he says is turned up upon entering and down on retiring; the Countersign, same or a wave of the hand; the Password, **Confidence**; the Alarm, two raps; the Grip, shake hands in ordinary manner, then press each other's forefinger, whole length of finger, gently, hooking the forefingers slightly as the hands are withdrawn.

Chancellor Commander.—"You being correct so far in the work of this Chivalric Rank, I will now instruct you in the following. The Sign of Recognition or Challenge Sign is:

SIGN OF RECOGNITION OR CHALLENGE SIGN, THIRD RANK.

Place left hand over the heart; right hand open, palm down and about the height of the hips, indicating the position your hands were in when you took the obligation.

The answer is the same, indicating the same, it being simply the position your hands were in when assuming the obligation of the First, or Initiatory Rank of Page.

The Voting Sign is:

VOTING SIGN.

Clench the left hand and raise it about as high as the eyes.

The Semi-Annual Password, as its name indicates, and which is given at the outer door, (the Rank Passwords are not,) is*—

The Parry Sign is:

PARRY SIGN.

Bring sword to a "Present" and swing point from right to left as if to parry or ward off a blow. When sign is completed the right hand will be about a foot from the body and the sword will point about two feet in front of left foot.

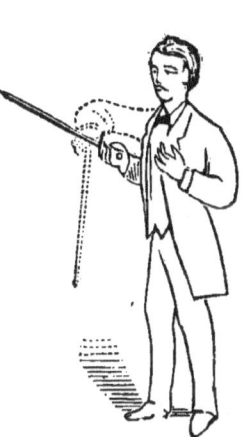

The Grand Honors are given thus:

GRAND HONORS.

Place the left hand on the heart and sword at a "present."

SUPREME HONORS.

Given like Grand Honors except that left forearm is held horizontal, extending directly forward, elbow at side, with hand open and palm up.

---

*The Semi-Annual Pass Word for the last half of 1878 (July to Jan.) was "Be United."

Chancellor Commander.—"I will here state to you that no signs, passwords, or other instruction given you in this Order, will be of any avail or assistance to you, when in anywise transgressing the laws of the country or reputable rules of society; neither are they binding upon you when given, made or sent to you by any other member of the Order guilty of these offences; this you will invariably bear in mind.

"Your close attention is always asked to the manner in which the Altar is arranged when you enter the Lodge, and to which your notice has been called before, as by it you will always give the correct sign of the rank in which it may be working, and thereby prevent disclosing that to others which they may not be legally entitled to, therefore, I will now explain them to you. In the First, or Initiatory Rank of Page, it is with the Book open, two swords crossed underneath, and handles towards the Chancellor Commander; in the Second, or Armorial Rank of Esquire, the same, except that the swords are on top of the Book of Law, while in the Third, or Chivalric Rank of Knight there is but one sword to be seen, which lies on top of the Book, diagonally across it, and with the handle toward the Vice Chancellor's station. These you will please charge your memory with, and thereby prevent mistakes occurring.

"Brother Brown, you have now passed through the Third, or Chivalric Rank of Knight, and the highest that can be given you in this Lodge. The motto thereof is **Bravery**, you have been severely tested, and passed the ordeal unscathed, exemplifying in part your confidence in and willingness to adhere to all lawful mandates. **Bravery** is defined as courage, heroism, undaunted spirit, intrepidity and gallantry, though there are other meanings to the term. There is a moral as well as a physical courage; the lesson inculcated in this instance embraces them both. You are expected to be brave and courageous in upholding the rights of a brother, maintaining the dignity of the Order, or its tenets of Friendship,.Charity and Benevolence, and though the uninitiated and skeptical person should deride, condemn or mock, ever stand ready to defend it and them from slur or sarcasm; not that they would in any manner take from it or its teachings the honor due, but let the world know that any shaft aimed thereat is as though received by yourself. Aiding thus in upholding our rights, usages and customs as a chivalric order, you strengthen and sustain our glorious principles, and more closely unite yourself with those who are linked together in the holy ties of brotherly love. Courage enables you to encounter difficulties and dangers with firmness and without fear of depression of spirits; it is also a constituent part of fortitude, which implies patience to bear continued suffering. Constitutional courage often forsakes its possessor in the hour of danger, but courage which arises from a sense of duty, like that of the noble Pythias when addressing the tyrant Dionysius:

"As thou'rt a husband and father, hear me—
Let Damon go and see his wife and child
Before he dies—for four hours respite him—
Put me in chains; plunge me into his dungeon
As pledge for his return; do this—but this—
And may the gods themselves build up thy greatness
As high as their own heaven."

"Courage like this, when coupled with friendship, acts uniformly. Brother Knight John Brown, I have no fear but that you will prove yourself in like manner Friendly, Cautious and Brave—ever ready to extend the strong hand of fellowship toward your brethren, and to stand by the courageous.

(Sometimes the Candidate is here catechised in reference to the Signs, Countersign, Pass Word, alarm on entering, the Grip etc. of the degree. See page 54.)

Chancellor Commander.—"Keeper of Records and Seal, you will now present the Roster of this Lodge to Brother Knight John Brown for enrollment."

Keeper of Records and Seal presents the book, with Constitution and By-Laws in it, kept for that purpose; the Knight signs his name, and enters his residence or address.

Chancellor Commander.—"Master at Arms, you will now face the newly charged Brother Knight to the Lodge, and clothe him in the proper regalia or insignia of the Third, or Chivalric and Honorable Rank of Knight."

Master at Arms.—"Chancellor Commander your orders have been obeyed."

Chancellor Commander (two raps).—"Officers, members and visitors of —— Lodge, No. —, Knights of Pythias, permit me to introduce to you Brother Knight John Brown, who has been regularly initiated in the First, Initiatory or Page's, proved in the Second, Armorial or Esquire's, and fully charged in the Third, Chivalric or Knight's Rank of this Order, in the usual ritualistic and ceremonial form, [examined in accordance with the law—should such be the case. This examination referred to is frequently and in some Lodges usually omitted], and enrolled as a member of —— Lodge, No. —, Knights of Pythias. Brethren, join with me in extending a hearty, sincere and chivalric welcome to our Brother Knight." (One rap.)

All gather around and shake hands.

Chancellor Commander. — "Lodge will be at ease until the sound of the gavel at the Chancellor Commander's station.

REMARKS ON THIRD RANK.

Of the injurious effects produced by the grand titles used by the order of Knights, we give the result of the opinion of the citizens of the United States as expressed in their National Constitution. Sec. 9: paragraph 7.

"No title of nobility shall be granted by the United States; and no person holding any office of profit or trust under them, shall without the consent of Congress, accept of any present, emolument, office or title of any kind whatever, from any King, Prince or foreign State."

The offensive boasting of *Bravery* taught in the third degree must be repugnant to every truly brave and well balanced mind.

"Though I were perfect yet would I not know my Soul." Job 9 ;21
"Where is boasting then? It is excluded." Rom. 3; 27.

In the last days when perilous times come men shall be "boasters" * * * See 2 Tim. 3: 1, 2.

The bravery test in the third degree, reminds us of a story illustrating the estimate placed on such unnecessary tests of courage by a genuine Knight of the olden time.

He with his lady love were seated together witnessing a fight of furious, hungry wild beasts in the arena below. The lady's glove fell into the arena. Said she, if you are loving and brave, bring me my glove. His pride led him to show his courage by entering the fearful arena and recovering the glove amidst shouts of applause from the crowds of shallow spectators ranged around. But the generous impulses of his soul were so severely shocked by the criminal wickedness and want of sensibility of a request to jeopardize his life for the recovery of a glove that he was constrained to show his scorn for such a spirit by throwing the glove into the lady's face and leaving her for ever.

The deceit connected with the bravery test aggravates rather than lessens the contemptible nature of the spike farce in the third rank.

Can any candid, noble nature uphold an institution after becoming aware that it systematically practices such chicanery ?

INITIATION.

Amended, Perfected and Amplified Ancient and Chivalric Form
OF THE
THIRD RANK, KNIGHTS OF PYTHIAS.

NOTE:—This Rank and the "regular" Third Rank are substantially one; only differing in the mode of conferring. No man who has taken either of them will receive the other third rank.

The Perfected and Amplified Rank is conferred in but a few wealthy lodges, because of the great expense attending the purchase of the apparatus for conferring it.

The Esquire is taken to the ante-room when he is instructed by the Master at Arms to say, in answer to any direct interrogatory made of him, "By what right does he make this demand?" the answer will be, "By that of being a brave man," or else get the candidate to authorize him—the Master at Arms—to do so for him, after which he is blindfolded, the shield put on his left fore-arm as in the preceding Rank; he is then conducted to the inner door, upon which there is no shield; the Master at Arms gives two raps, which are answered in the same manner from within, and the wicket is opened.

Inner Guard.—"Who comes here? Who dares to interrupt the proceedings of this Lodge while working in the Third, or Chivalric Rank of Knight?"

Master at Arms.—"Esquire John Brown, who having received the First, or Initiatory Rank of Page, been proved in the Second or Armorial Rank of Esquire, and passing a fair ballot, now declares himself a **Brave** man, and as such demands admittance to this Lodge of the Third, or Chivalric Rank of Knight."

Inner Guard (closes wicket.)—"Chancellor Commander, there is without an Esquire who has received the First or Initiatory Rank of Page, been proved in the Second or Armorial Rank of Esquire, and now demands admittance to this Lodge of the Third or Chivalric Rank of Knight."

Chancellor Commander.—"By what right does he make this demand?"

Inner Guard.—"By reason of having been initiated, proved, passing a fair ballot, and boasting himself a **Brave** man."

Chancellor Commander.—"Such being his pledge and demand and having attained the necessary preparatory Rank, it is my order as Chancellor Commander that you let him enter without further challenge."

The Master at Arms conducts the Esquire around the Castle Hall once and halts before the chair of the Chancellor Commander.

Master at Arms.—"Chancellor Commander, Esquire John Brown, who has been duly initiated as a Page, and proved as an Esquire, in this Chivalric Order, desires to receive the highest Rank conferred by this Lodge, by being instructed in the mysteries and passing through the ordeal that all brave Knights have done who have reached this summit of Pythian honors."

Chancellor Commander.—"Esquire, is this your demand?"

Candidate answers.

Chancellor Commander.—"Upon entering this Castle Hall as a Retainer, seeking the First or Initiatory Rank of Page, a requirement was exacted from and of you; do you remember what it was, and if so, will you state its nature?"

Candidate.—**Obedience.**"

Chancellor Commander.—"Brethren of the Knight's Rank, are you satisfied that the Esquire remembers and fully appreciates this requirement sufficient to advance him in our highest honors?"

(All.)—"We are."

Chancellor Commander.—"Upon attaining the First or Initiatory Rank of Page in this order, you were taught one great lesson. Do you remember what it was, and if so will you be kind enough to state the same?"

Candidate.—**"Friendship."**

Chancellor Commander.—"Brethren of the Knight's Rank, has the Esquire who demands advancement in our order merited as well as received your **Friendship.**"

(All.)—"He has."

Chancellor Commander.—"Upon reaching and being proved in the Second or Armorial Rank of Esquire of this order, you were taught another great lesson. Will you state what it was?"

Candidate.—**"Caution."**

Chancellor Commander.—"Brethren of the Knight's Rank, has

the Esquire who stands before you as a candidate for the Third or Chivalric Rank of Knight, proven himself, to the best of your knowledge and belief, obedient, prudent, cautious and watchful?"

(All.)—"He has."

Chancellor Commander.—"This being so, Esquire, I can see no just reason why you should not be permitted to proceed in this Chivalric Order; but it is my duty to inform you that your courage and confidence may be put to a severe test during the ceremonies through which you are about to pass, but should such be the will of those around you assembled, and if, as you declare in your demand, you are a **Brave** man, and will implicitly obey all the orders given you, and requirements exacted during its progress, no accident can possibly befall you. On the contrary, if you are not a man of iron nerve, or if you have made this demand from an unworthy motive, I tell you plainly and sincerely that I cannot be answerable for any **injury** you may receive. To assure you, however, that this Lodge, its officers and members fully appreciate your position, I will, as Chancellor Commander, state that the ordeal you may have to undergo is one, not only dangerous in character, but of a fearful nature. Should your vaunted bravery fail you at the crowning point of its consummation, by it we as an order prove and exemplify the fact as to whether you have been truthful in your former protestations of Friendship, such as was exhibited by Damon towards Pythias, or the Caution, though unwise, as shown by Lucullus in slaying his master's horse to preserve his life.

"Heretofore you have answered readily and promptly the interrogatories as made in the former and preceding grades of rank but the answers now to be given are of too serious a nature to be lightly made, and I would therefore ask your greatest consideration before so doing; but to give you a last opportunity to elect for yourself, I will state that it is not too late, if you so desire, to be escorted hence and permitted to retire, (pause). With the official assurance from me that no accident can befall an obedient and friendly person, who is not only cautious but a truly brave man, aspiring to the high rank of Knight, I ask, as Chancellor Commander, in the name of this Lodge, its officers and members around you assembled, do you still persist in your demand?"

Candidate answers.

Chancellor Commander.—"Are you willing to take upon your self a solemn and binding obligation to keep forever secret the mysteries of this Chivalric Rank of Knight?"

Candidate answers.

Chancellor Commander.—"Master at Arms, you will conduct the Esquire to our Prelate, who will administer the obligation of the Third and Chivalric Rank of Knighthood in this Order."

Master at Arms presents candidate before the Prelate at the Altar, opposite to and facing him.

Master at Arms.—"Prelate, by order of the Chancellor Com_mander of this Lodge, I present Esquire John Brown, who having been initiated as a Page and proved in the Second or Armorial Rank of Esquire, now declares himself a **Brave** man, and as such demands that he be obligated in the Third or Chivalric Rank of Knight in this Order."

Prelate.—"Esquire John Brown, do you declare yourself a **Brave** man, and make this demand of your own volition?"

Candidate answers.

Prelate.—"Master at Arms, why is he thus blindfolded?"

Master at Arms.—"That he might be conducted through this Castle Hall without being able to discover any of the secrets or ceremonies of the Knight Rank of our Order, should he fail to insist in his demands before the Chancellor Commander."

Prelate.—"Since the Esquire insists in his demands, you will remove the hoodwink, (which being done, the Prelate continues,) and place him in proper position, at the Altar, to take the obligation, by advancing his shield in placing his left hand on his left breast, over the heart, advancing his right foot, his right hand resting on the Book of Law and grasping the hilt of the Sword of Defence before him as if making a parry with the sword, in which position he will assume the obligation."

Master at Arms places candidate in proper position.

Chancellor Commander.—(Two raps.) Attention Knights.

Rise; form triangle and assist our Prelate in the administration of the solemn obligation. (See diagram.)

ADMINISTERING OBLIGATION THIRD OR CHIVALRIC RANK OF KNIGHT

Candidate stands at altar as described, the prelate standing opposite, the Master at Arms behind and to the left of the candidate.

The Knights form a triangle with the Chancellor Commander at its apex, the Vice Chancellor at the right corner and the Past Chancellor at the left corner.

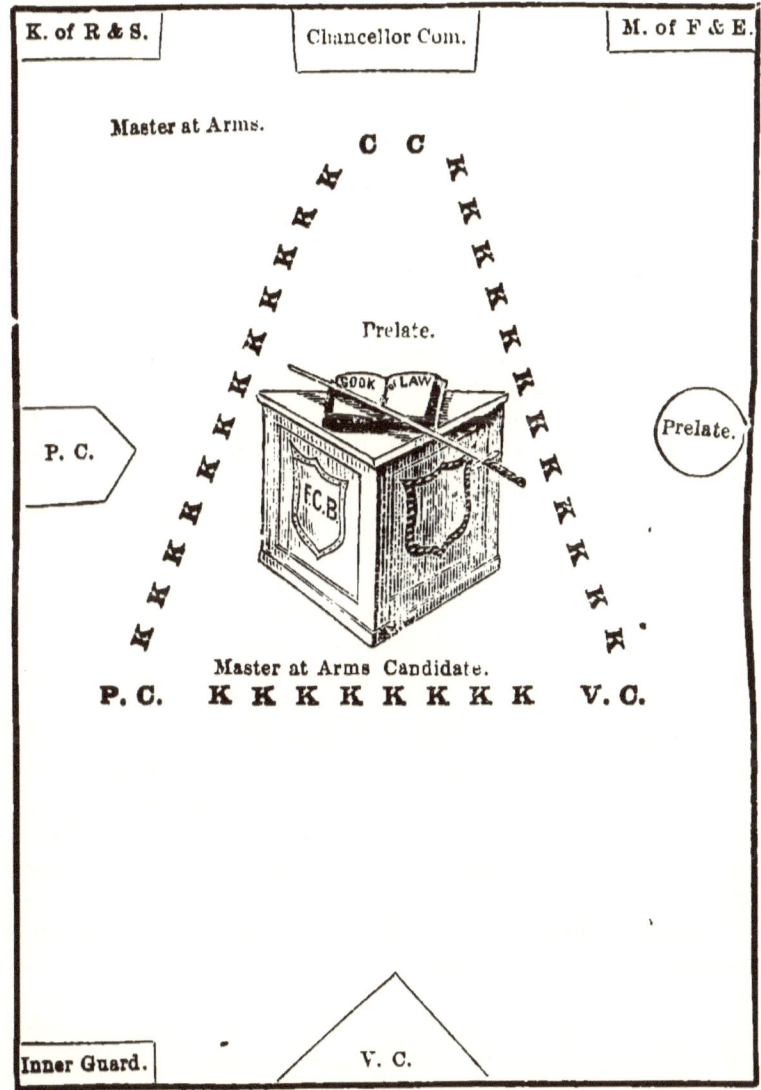

K. of R & S.　　Chancellor Com.　　M. of F & E.

Master at Arms.

C C

Prelate.

P. C.

Prelate.

F.C.B.

Master at Arms Candidate.

P. C.　K K K K K K K K　V. C.

Inner Guard.　　V. C.

The triangle being formed, the Chancellor Commander will order;

Chancellor Commander.—Attention Knights! Handle swords; draw swords; carry arms.

(Prelate rising goes to and enters the head of the triangle, and assumes his position at the Altar, the Candidate and Master at Arms already having assumed theirs, when all being in their proper position, the Past Chancellor, Chancellor Commander and Vice Chancellor leave their stations and go to the corners at head and base of the triangle, when the Chancellor Commander orders "Rest!" and the Prelate proceeds.)

Obligation Amended, Perfected and Amplified Third Rank.

"(You will now repeat after me.) I, (your name) do most solemnly and sincerely promise and declare, under the penalties of my former obligations, that I will never reveal, directly or indirectly, any of the signs, tokens or mysteries of this Rank of **Bravery**, or those of any other Rank of the Knights of Pythias, to any person not properly authorized by this, or a Lodge working under the control of a regularly constituted Grand Lodge, recognized by the Supreme Lodge Knights of Pythias of the World, to receive the same; except it be a just and lawful Knight, whom I shall know to be legally entitled to receive the same, or within the Castle Hall of a just and regularly constituted Lodge, subordinate to the Supreme Lodge, Knights of Pythias of the World.

"I further promise and declare, never to communicate, by word, syllable, letter, sign or character, the semi-annual password to any person, save and except the proper officers within a Lodge, or in course of duty, acting in capacity of Chancellor Commander, Grand Chancellor or his deputy, or Supreme Chancellor or his deputy.

"I further promise to obey all orders that may be given me, emanating from the Supreme, Grand, this or any other Lodge of this Order of which I may become a member, or any competent authority issuing the same, so long as they do not conflict with my political or religious liberty. And if I ever, by word or sign, expose the secret work or ceremonies of this Order, in an unauthorized manner, or fail in any of my obligations, may I suffer all the anguish and torments possible for man to suffer. All this I promise and declare, without any mental reservation whatever. So help me God, and keep me steadfast."

"Prelate.—"Esquire John Brown, in testimony of your sincerity, you will now kiss the Book that is open before you, which is our Book of Law, the Holy Bible." (Kisses the book.)

Prelate.—"Esquire, you have now taken the obligation that ties you to us, and I hail you as an aspirant to the honors due to a Knight of this Order. You must ever remember your obligation, and the purpose of your shield in the Second or Armorial Rank of Esquire in this Order. You have seen how easily you might have fallen into an error, but for the interposition of a brother. Let the solemnity of that occurrence be ever present in your mind and emblazoned upon your shield and memory, to stimulate you to fulfill and keep inviolate every obligation taken by you. The obligation to which you have just subscribed, imposes a condition to obey all orders which may be given you, so long as they do not conflict with your civil or religious liberty. You have also stated in this Lodge that you are a man of courage. That assertion remains yet to be proven; My friend have confidence and all is well. Farewell! (Prelate steps aside from the Altar, face about to the Chancellor Commander and says:)

Prelate.—"Chancellor Commander, the Esquire has been obligated and cautioned.

Chancellor Commander (from his position at the head of the triangle.)—"Master at Arms, conduct hence this Esquire, equip him as becomes his rank and give him courteous guidance to the "Ten in Council," who shall for us decide what test of bravery the Esquire bears.

Attention, Knights! Break files at center base of triangle. [The four files break to the rear—(see diagram)—candidate and Master at Arms pass out—which being done, the Chancellor Commander orders:] Close triangle; return swords; about face; to posts march; be seated.

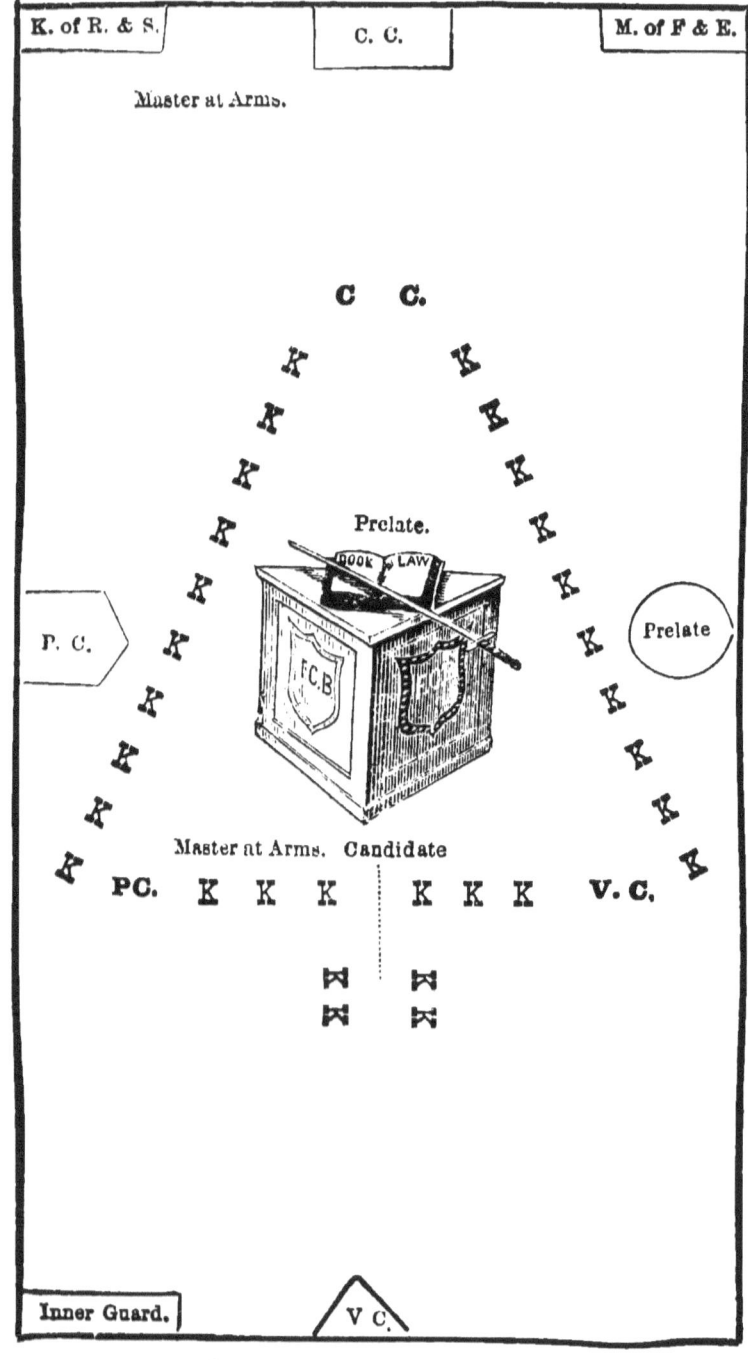

K. of R. & S.

C. C.

M. of F & E.

Master at Arms.

C C.

Prelate.

BOOK LAW

Prelate

P. C.

FC.B

Master at Arms. Candidate

PC. K K K K K K V. C.

Inner Guard.

V C.

Master at Arms conducts candidate to ante-room, relieves him of his shield, clothes him with the uniform Belt of the Order, without sword or scabbard, and puts sandals on his feet. The Council of Ten being in readiness, of which he is notified by a single rap on the door by the "Warder of the Gate," the Master at Arms approaches and gives several loud raps in quick succession.

THE COUNCIL OF TEN

is composed of the following personages:

King, represented by the Prelate.

"Warder of the Gate," represented by the Inner Guard.

"Nine Councillors," known respectively as "First Councillor," "Second Councillor," etc.

The Council is held in the Lodge-room, or some chamber specially prepared. If the former, the lower end should be occupied by the Council, the King being seated in the Vice Chancelior's chair, facing the Councillors, who are seated in a semi-circle about him. The King and Councillors should be clothed in full uniform of the Order, or in suits of armor—all being either visored or masked.

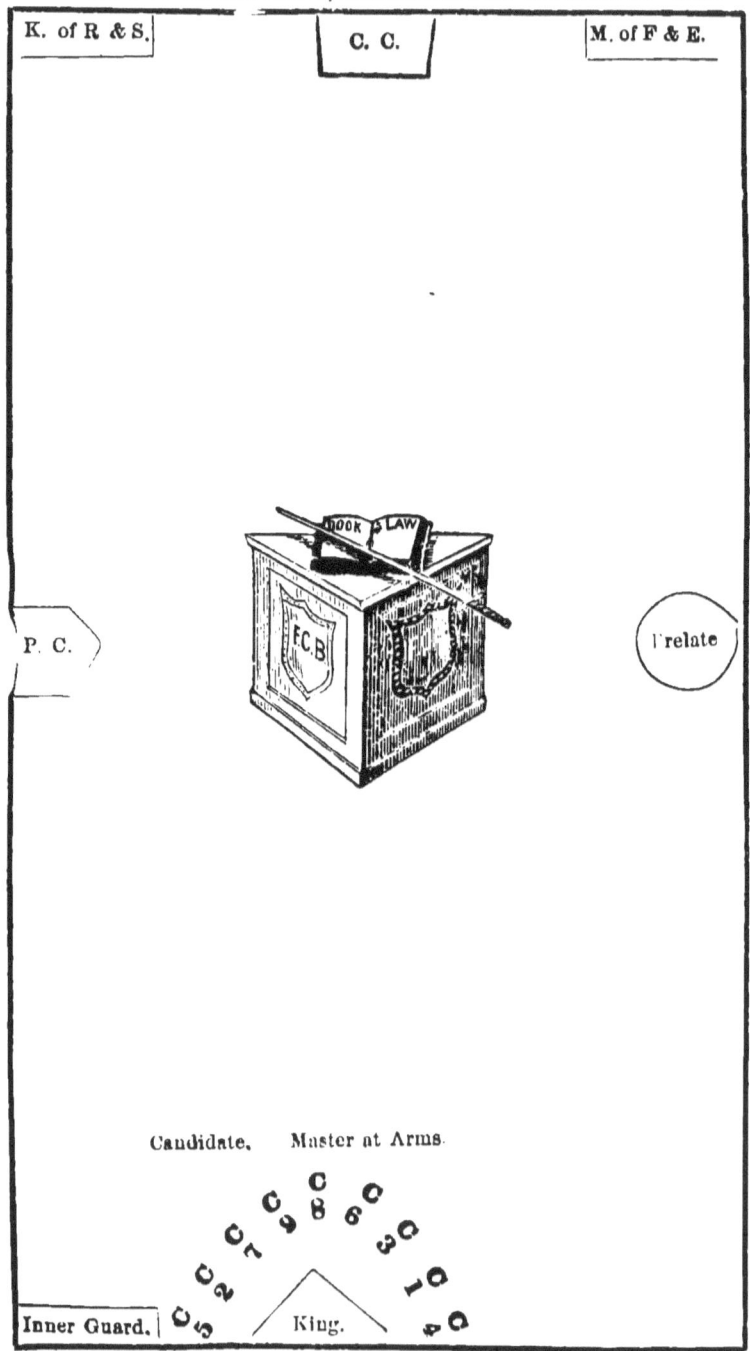

The Knights and visitors are seated as usual around the room, masked and in black robes or uniform of the order.

Councillors in full armor or uniform, seated, with visors down or masked.

CEREMONIES IN OPENING COUNCIL OF TEN.

Enter King of Council, (announced by the Warder of the Gate, "The King!") Councillors all arise and remain standing, King ascends the throne, raising his visor.

King.—"Brethren, with knightly courtesy I greet you. Are all here?

Warder of the Gate (saluting).—"They are, most knightly King."

King.—"Up visors, gentlemen, that you and I may know each one the other."

(All raise their visors, or unmask.)

King.—"I see here now the nine true Knights who, with myself, do constitute the "Ten," from whose decision there is no appeal; whose edicts once sent forth are to the inmates of our Castle Hall established law. Questions of deep import exercise our mind, and in due time the matter shall be cognizant to all. I now declare this Council formed, and on my honor as a Knight, I pledge myself to secrecy, swearing the same by my extended sword."

King draws and extends his sword, and Knight Councillors drawing, cross their swords thereon, (or if unarmed, extend and lay their right hand thereon,) and say,

"And I," "and I," "and I," etc.

King.—"Amen."

(King withdraws his sword returns it to the scabbard, then takes his seat.)

King.—"Be seated. Warder, make fast our gates. Knights, in view of those who may the presence of this Council seek, 'twere well that each one drop the visor o'er his face."

(Loud knocking at the inner door.)

King.—"What means this boisterous clamor at our gate? One of you away and bring us tidings of the cause."

Warder of the Gate goes to the door, raises wicket, through which he receives a parchment; closes wicket and going to the center of the Council circle and directly in front of the King, reports:

Warder of the Gate.—"Most knightly King, without I found a brave and valiant Knight, leading an Esquire in pilgrim garb,for whom he seeks the right to wear the high prized honor of the golden spur, and sends this voucher of his equity."

(Hands parchment to King, who peruses the same and says:)

King.—"As he is vouched for by our well tried friend as being made of honest, manly stuff, there stands no reason to withhold the boon, if we shall find him as endorsement states, a brave and worthy man. Admit him to the presence of the Ten."

The Warder of the Gate goes to and opens the door. Master at Arms with candidate enters and assumes a position outside semi-circle, at the center and opposite the King.

Master at Arms.—"Most knightly King and brothers of our band, I here present an Esquire I have known, bearing an honest name among his fellow men, and being gifted with patrician soul he seeks to rise above the common herd and prove himself a man of iron nerve—a fit companion for these well tried knights."

King.—"At your request, and without waste of speech, I bid this Council on the test decide; asking the pilgrim if he still persist?"

Candidate.—"I do."

First Councillor (rising and addressing the King and Council.) —"I would decree that he be made to spring from off the summit of yon beetling cliff, down to the fretful waves that surge below." (Resumes his seat.)

Second Councillor (rising).—"That were to bid him spring to certain death; the quick descent would filch his necessary wind, and we might lose a valiant knight thereby: rather let us stretch his naked frame over a furnace of white heated coals, and if his lips are parted by a moan, vote him not fit to sit within our Hall." (Resumes his seat.)

Third Councillor (rising).—"The last named test were scarce less fatal than the one before, the chance of life depending on the briefness of the ordeal. In lieu of these, I do propose that he be made to leap upon a score of tempered spikes, set in a solid slab of living oak; and when they pierce his naked, tender feet, let each one prime his ears to catch the groaning of each new born pain." (Resumes his seat.)

Fourth Councillor (who is seated at one extreme end of semi-circle, rises and addresses King alone.)—"Most knightly King, methought I saw a shade of hesitation passing o'er the pilgrim's face; aye, more, I'll wager me it was most arrant fear, and by my spurs I doubt he hath this courage that he claims." (Resumes his seat.)

Fifth Councillor (seated at the other extreme of semicircle, rising and addressing the King and Council.)—"Aye, fear it was, most certainly, for with my eyes I saw him quail, and cast a troubled glance around as if for pity, which we as knightly councillors know naught of, save for distress and those of gentler sex." (Resumes his seat.)

King (to candidate, earnestly).—"It grieves me much that one so recommended, and deemed by his good guide both resolute and brave, should by a tremor show his dread of test. Pilgrim Esquire, ere you can wear the insignia of a Knight—the golden spur, denotive of your manhood and true courage—your feet must tread the drear and ofttimes dangerous path to Pythian honors, and you must show by acts that wear the native hue of bravery that you are worthy of the rank to which we can advance you. Despite your show of fear, you cannot now withdraw, but on the choosing of these Knights, must go where they dictate— and go alone, save that old Pluto bear you company, and as a guardian he were worse than none.

Sixth Councillor (rising, draws his sword, presents, and after the words "Most knightly King," comes to a carry.)—"Most knightly King, I would vouchsafe a word on this poor pilgrim's part, telling my story with all briefness that I may. At one time in the rage of battle, by a foeman's lance my horse and I were parted 'gainst our wills; and as I lay both spent and bleeding on the ground, a youth, a simple Page, passed by in course of duty, and looking back he saw me helpless on our mother earth, the life blood oozing from my gaping wounds: quickly he tore his doublet into strips and staunched their flow, then bore me off to safe and shady nook, and by his gentle care I live to-day. In view of this I registered a vow to help a Page, aye, Esquire or Knight, who needed aid, to succor him from ill; and 'fore this

Esquire I renew my vow, and proffer him protection if he crave it." (Moves towards the candidate and remains standing, as if to assume his part in whatever it may be decreed he shall do.)

Seventh Councillor (rising and addressing the King).—"Most knightly King, the words just spoken honor him who gave them utterance, and yet it were not well that one so high in rank, so great on field of battle, so loved among his brother knights, should risk his life for this' Esquire, with whom we have but slight acquaintance, and who, I doubt, can ever take the place of one so tried as our brave brother. Who wears the spurs should win them, and thus for caution's sake, and for prudential reasons I would urge that this man carve his way to the high honor he sees fit to claim. It would most seemly be (turning to the Council), that one and all reject, without debate, the offer made."

Council (all rising).—"We do reject it." (Council are all seated except Sixth Councillor.)

King.—" 'Tis well, and be it understood, most valiant Knight, that you remain, (Sixth Councillor resumes his seat) while you Esquire, will win alone the spurs you seek to wear. And now brave Knights, by favor of our friend, let each man cast his lot; taking the colors as the tests were named—blue for the first, yellow the next and red the third."

Master at Arms distributes to King and each Councillor three slips of paper, blue, yellow and red respectively; then collects them in a suitable manner, each one depositing his red paper and retaining the other two. Master at Arms presents receptacle to King, who examines the ballot and says:

King.—"The third is chosen. Away with him and bid old Pluto put him to the test."

Master at Arms saluting King with sword, retires with candidate.

King (rising to his feet, drawing his sword and coming to a carry).—"By virtue of my will this Council stands dissolved."

The Council rise to their feet, and opening at the center, swing back and close up their lines, facing inward, at the same time drawing their swords, bringing them to a carry, and as the King moves down, present arms all together, (or if unarmed, make military salute). The King passes between the two ranks, and arriving at the end of the lines, faces about and salutes, when he orders:

King.—"Carry arms—about face—to your posts march, and be seated."

[This ends the ceremony. See diagram.]

DISSOLVING COUNCIL OF TEN.

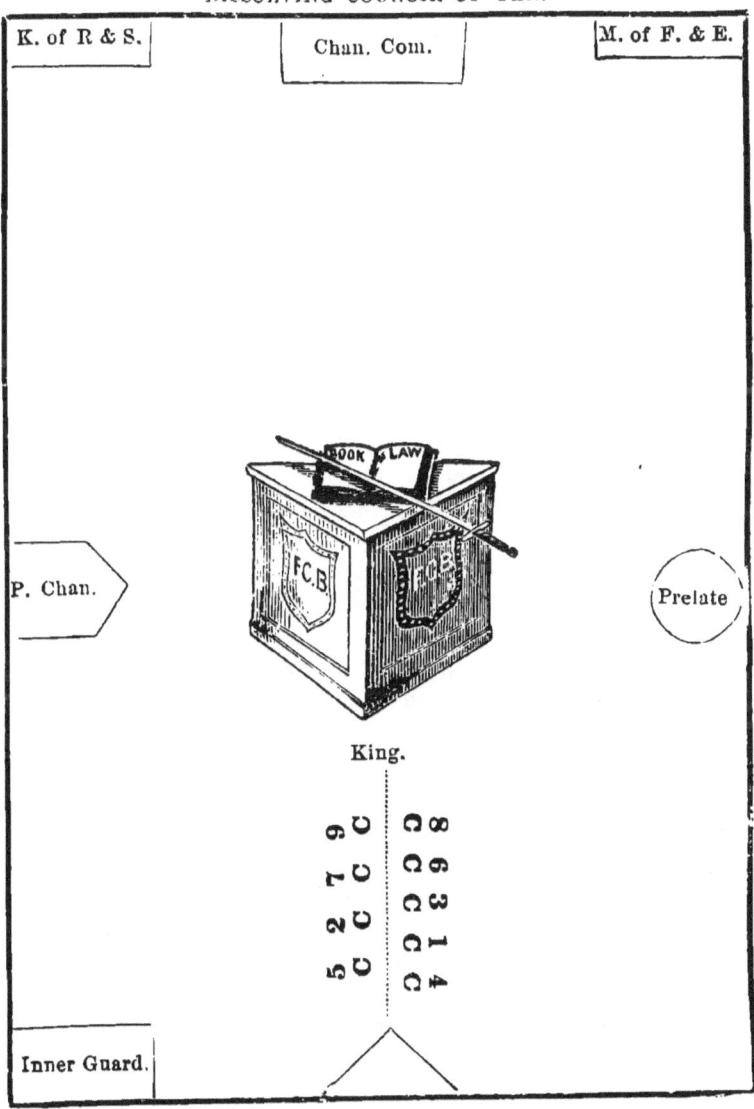

The Lodge-room is darkened, made as nearly as possible to represent a wilderness. To the right of the Chancellor Commanders's station is an elevation representing a mound, on which is laid a complete skeleton,(or its representation.) On the right of the Vice Chancellor is placed a mock cauldron, in which is burned some red fire, round which are gathered some of the Knights robed in black and masked, apparently wrangling over the contents. The cue for igniting the red fire and grouping around the cauldron, is the utterance by Pluto, of the following words: "I left him there to fatten up the bloodhounds of this wilderness."

Pluto is seated in the center of the room, dressed in a suit of silver mail, cavalier cloak of black, trimmed with silver lace, suspended from left shoulder; helmet similar to that worn by the herald Mercury; and sword. [Pluto is represented by the Past Chancellor or by some other qualified person.]

Master at Arms enters with candidate, clothed as when before the Council of Ten, walks slowly towards the center of the room and halts about one-half way between the door and Pluto.

Pluto (looking up).—"Who dares to break the stillness of eternal night by wandering past the limits of the earth to my most dread abode? Beats there a heart with slow and measured pulse when standing at the gate of Pluto's wild domain?"

Master at Arms.—"Imperial Prince, behold a well-tried 'Squire who craves the honors of his knightly spurs, and boasts himself a brave, courageous man. Ere we accord this honor that he craves, we do appeal to you, the potent king of this most barren waste, to test him to the quick, and if he lacks the courage that he boasts, let his flesh blister in yon furnace heat, till dropping from the bones, it leaves a calcined record on the road, to warn others of the coward's fate."

Master at Arms, leaving the candidate standing there, retires out of sight.

Pluto (rising and approaching candidate).—"Welcome, thou denizen of earth. If thou art brave I will conduct thee safe, and recommend thee for thy knightly spurs; but if thy cheek show but a tinge of that white-livered hue that I have called the countersign of fear; if thy strong limbs but for a moment shake and tremble like an aspen in the road, bid then farewell to earth! (Takes candidate by the right arm.) Come, let us go, and as you tread, beware! for deadly adders swarm in your path, whose foul envenomed fangs would quickly still the beating of your heart."

Stoops as if catching something from the ground, and exhibits an imitation snake, that he had concealed on his person.

Pluto.—"See! here is one, that springing from the pregnant ground would, but for the power I hold, have fastened on your flesh; and still another (other snakes are seen on the floor that they are likely to tread on) creeps around my foot. Be brave, and all is well!"

[An imitation mound with skeleton thereon.]

"Look on yon mound; there lies the framework of a coward soul, who wandering round with me as you do now, trembled to hear the howling of wild beasts. This show of fear invoked my wrath, and with a swoop of my avenging sword, I left him there to fatten up the bloodhounds of this wilderness."

[The cauldron is set on fire.]

"Ah! yonder leaps the red and lurid flame! (A mock cauldron with colored fire, surrounded by masked knights robed in black, is seen at further end of Lodge-room.) Note how it licks around that coward's bones, and boils the water of his stagnant blood! My sable band hold royal feast over a victim that I slew last night; see how they quarrel o'er his livered blood, and wrangle for a dish full of his brains! Ere yet the hand of death had stopped the twitching of his livid limbs, and while he writhed beneath the fatal blow, they plucked his hair out by the roots, twisted his nails from out their fleshy bed and rubbed saltpetre on his gaping wounds.

"Ho! one of you, come quickly hither and produce the test!"

[Vice Chancellor, who is robed in black and masked, approaches and presents the test. Pluto takes it.]

"I have provided here, by order of the 'Ten,' a goodly combination of tough wood and steel; take it yourself that you may see the points."

[Hands it to candidate, who takes and examines it.]

Pluto.—"Of its keen sharpness are you well assured?" (Pluto tries it with his sword.)

Candidate answers.

Pluto to Vice Chancellor.—"Begone, and place it on the testing spot!"

[Vice Chancellor takes it from the candidate, carries it to the testing spot, where it is put in position in full view of the candidate, and the change made by the Vice Chancellor at the proper time and quietly as possible.]

[Pluto, in an unconcerned and careless manner, turns the candidate with his back to the testing spot, and placing his hands upon the candidate's shoulders, looks him square in the eyes to attract his attention while saying:]

Pluto.—"Come, let me gaze into your eyes, those well springs of the soul, from which outflash the hidden secrets of the heart! When Adam fell from his primeval bliss, tempted by me through unsuspecting Eve, I made him deaf to Gabriel's cautioning tongue, lest he might stop, considering, on the brink, and waxing brave, upset my plans for peopling this wild waste. Thus much is left of my angelic mould, that to the brave I give my knightly hand to bear them safe o'er this unhallowed soil: but to the man of weak and reedy nerve I leave the wooing of my untamed imps that seek an introduction to his blood."

[At this moment the curtain at the chair of the Chancellor Commander is drawn aside and the Chancellor Commander is seen, dressed in a scarlet robe, with a white cross upon his breast, a gilt crown upon his head and a gilt cross, as a sceptre, in his hand. Pluto, turning, sees him, (trembling,) says:]

Pluto.—"Before that awful emblem of my great defeat I bow in mute despair, and leaving you in guardianship of him whose word to me is law, I vanish from your sight."

[Pluto retires out of sight, as noiselessly as possible, and lays aside his robes, etc.]

Chancellor Commander descending from and leaving his station, takes the candidate by the left arm, so as to keep him away from the test while the board with iron spikes is slily replaced with one with rubber spikes, addresses him while leading him around finally to the testing spot, as follows:

Chancellor Commander.—"Esquire, it was decreed by the Grand Council who essayed you here, that as a proof of your obedience and unflinching nerve, you jump with naked feet upon that instrument of torture. I bid you now make bare each tender foot, and at the instant that I orders give, leap on those bristling points."

[Master at Arms assists him to take off his sandals and ascend the eminence.]

Chancellor Commander, (to the Knights).—"Come, one and all, and bear him witness in the act, and if he fail, conduct ye as ye will."

[Knights assemble around without further command, with swords at a carry. All being ready, the Chancellor Commander continuing, says:]

Chancellor Commander.—"Now, if you are a brave and steel-souled man, Leap down!"

[In case he refuses, after a third command, the Chancellor Commander steps forward, puts his foot on it and then requires the candidate to do it; both feet must go on.]

Chancellor Commander (returning to his station).—"Attention Knights! return swords; about face; posts march; be seated."

[After the ceremonies, the candidate puts on his sandals and is conducted to the station of the Chancellor Commander, the costumes of each having been laid aside, or not, as may be desired.]

Chancellor Commander (to candidate).—"My friend, the ceremonies you have passed through were not conceived in idle sport to trifle with your feelings, but to convey a practical lesson to your mind in a manner so impressive as not to be easily effaced. You was brought into the presence of our armed council to remind you that good men are always clad in the bright armor of Truth and Virtue, from which the shafts of Vice and Falsehood fall harmlessly to the ground.

"You was vouched for by a friend to show the necessity of an upright life if we would enter into the habitations of the good beyond the grave. A lesson of Friendship was given you when standing alone and unprotected, by one to you unknown, who volunteered to bear, in your behalf, the test on which the Council might decide; but Caution to the rescue came and bade you go alone, lest we might lose the counsels of a well-tried Knight, for the rash promptings of a reckless but well-meaning mind.

"Then you was led through a wilderness, to remind you of life's journey; that we have no abiding city here, nor is the prospect sufficiently inviting to induce us to seek to wander here forever, even if we could.

"You was beset by snakes and adders to remind you of the trials and temptations of life; and in the fleshless form exhibited to you, you saw the penalty of Cowardice. Such is the punishment that awaits the soul that lacks the moral courage to stand bravely out, catching the shafts of Error upon the shield of Purity, and hewing Falsehood with the sword of Truth.

"You was then shown a scene indicative of the evil passions of man—evincing his readiness to rejoice in the downfall of his neighbor. The sudden vanishing of your conductor before the symbol of the cross, was to convey to your mind that there is a time when the evil doer will blanch before the stern face of justice, although his wickedness may seem to prosper for a season.

"Lastly, you was led to a place where your faith was put to the extremest test; you was there taught a lesson of obedience, but greater than all, you was shown that if you have only the moral heroism and stamina to face manfully the dangers that apparently surround you, you will find them mere shadows that vanish at the first blow.

"Such are the moral convictions we have striven to print indelibly on your mind, and we trust that your intercourse with the world at large will prove the lessons have not been in vain.

"Master at Arms, conduct our friend to the chair of the Vice Chancellor for further insight to our mysteries." (Master at Arms does so.)

Master at Arms (to Vice Chancellor).—"Obedient to command, Vice Chancellor, I present this candidate to you to be instructed in our secret work."

[If he obeyed command to jump on the spikes the Vice Chancellor says:]

Vice Chancellor.—"As a brave man I extend you cordial greeting, and now proceed to give you knowledge of our secret work, that you may know that he who wears the spurs has fairly won them"

[If he was not obedient the Vice Chancellor says:]

Vice Chancellor.—"As a brave and obedient man I cannot give you cordial greeting, yet will, in consideration of the many trials you have undergone, proceed to give you knowledge of our secret work, that you may know that he who wears the spurs should fairly win them."

SIGN OF BRAVERY OR COURTESY, THIRD RANK.

Form a triangle with forearms extending horizontally from you, points of fingers and thumbs together and spread out; heel of hands about five inches apart. See cut. This is called the visor sign.

VISOR SIGN ON ENTERING LODGE.

On entering to salute the Chancellor Commander, raise visor so as to touch the breast with the forefingers, the thumbs pointing downward. Hands are then separated and with a gentle wave are brought to the side.

VISOR SIGN ON RETIRING FROM LODGE.

On retiring approach the Altar, face the Chancellor Commander and turn the visor (hands) down, so that the thumbs point up and the fingers down and then bring hands to side with a gentle wave.

The Countersign, given by the Chancellor Commander, is same as sign or a wave of the hand. The Password, given at the inner door, is **Confidence.** The Alarm at the inner door is two raps. The Grip is given in this manner :

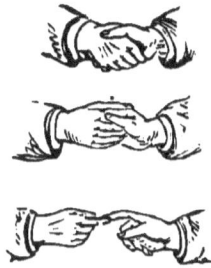

GRIP, THIRD RANK.

Take each other by the right hand as for ordinary hand shake. When withdrawing hands press each other's forefinger with thumb and forefinger, gently, the whole length of finger, slightly crooking the ends of the forefingers and hooking or **pressing** them together at the points.

Vice Chancellor.—"Master at Arms, you will now conduct our newly tried and instructed brother to the Chancellor Commander for final examination, instruction and enrollment on the roster of this Lodge, as having that Rank. (He does so.)

Master at Arms.—"Chancellor Commander, by direction of the Vice Chancellor of this Lodge, I present to you Brother John Brown, who has been instructed in the sign, countersign, password and grip of the Third or Chivalric Rank of Knight, for final examination, instruction and enrollment on the roster of this Lodge as having that Rank."

Chancellor Commander.—"Brother John Brown, as an evidence of the attention paid to the instruction already given you, you will be kind enough to satisfy me that you are in possession of the sign

Candidate gives the Visor Sign which he says is turned up on entering and down on retiring; the Countersign, same or a wave of the hand; the Password, **Confidence**; the Alarm, two raps; the Grip, shake hands in ordinary manner, then press each other's forefinger, whole length of finger, gently, hooking the forefingers slightly as the hands are withdrawn.

Chancellor Commander.—"Master at Arms, repair with our friend to the centre of our Castle Hall; place him in due position to be dubbed a Knight."

[Master at Arms places candidate in centre of hall, and causes him to kneel upon the right knee near the altar.]

Master at Arms.—"Chancellor Commander your orders have been obeyed."

Chancellor Commander.—"Attention, Knights! (all rise) Handle swords; draw swords; carry arms; forward and form triangle around candidate!" (See diagram, page 63.)

[Knights, with swords at "carry," surround the candidate on three sides, forming, as near as possible, a triangle. The Chancellor Commander approaches and strikes candidate with the flat of his sword on right shoulder three times, saying:]

Chancellor Commander.—"In the name of the Order Universal (one rap) and by power in me vested (one rap) as Chancellor Commander of this Lodge, (one rap) I bid thee rise and stand erect a Pythian Knight, (candidate rises) and in the presence of your conferes, I command you to be invested with the spurs your rank now entitles you to wear."

[Master at Arms invests candidate with a spur on each heel.]

Chancellor Commander.—"Attention, Knights! Present arms! (if armed, if not) Salute!"

[Knights present swords, (if armed,) if not, salute, by bringing right hand to head as if making a military salute.]

Chancellor Commander (returning to his station).—"Carry arms; return swords; about face; to your posts march!" (Knights march to their ordinary places in Lodge room.)

Chancellor Commander.—"Knights! about face; be seated!"

[The candidate and Master at Arms remain standing in centre of hall.]

Chancellor Commander.—"Master at Arms, you will present the newly tried and made brother at the Chancellor Commander's station." (He does so.)

Chancellor Commander.—"Knight John Brown, you have now passed through the Third or Chivalric Rank of Knight, and the highest that can be given you in this Lodge. The motto thereof is **Bravery**, you have been severely tested, and passed the ordeal unscathed, exemplifying in part your confidence in and willingness to adhere to all lawful mandates. **Bravery** is defined as courage, heroism, undaunted spirit, intrepidity and gallantry though there are other meanings to the term. There is a moral as well as a physical courage; the lesson inculcated in this instance embraces them both. You are expected to be brave and courageous in upholding the rights of a brother; maintaining the dignity of the order, or its tenets of Friendship, Charity and Benevolence, and though the uninitiated and skeptical person should deride, condemn or mock, ever stand ready to defend it and them from slur or sarcasm; not that they would in any manner take from it or its teachings the honor due, but let the world know that any shaft aimed thereat is as though received by yourself. Aiding thus in upholding our rights, usages and customs as a chivalric order, you strengthen and sustain our glorious principles, and more closely unite yourself with those who are linked together in the holy ties of brotherly love. Courage enables you to encounter difficulties and dangers with firmness and without fear of depression of spirits; it is also a constituent part of fortitude, which implies patience to bear continued suffering. Constitutional courage often forsakes its possessor in the hour of danger, but courage which arises from a sense of duty, like that of the noble Pythias when addressing the tyrant Dionysius:"

"As thou'rt a husband and father, hear me—
Let Damon go and see his wife and child
Before he dies—for four hours respite him—
Put me in chains; plunge me into his dungeon
As pledge for his return; do this—but this—
And may the gods themselves build up thy greatness
As high as their own heaven."

"Courage like this, when coupled with friendship, acts uniformly.

"Brother Knight John Brown, I have no fear but that you will prove yourself in like manner, Friendly, Cautious and Brave —ever ready to extend the strong hand of fellowship toward your brethren, and to stand by the courageous. In token whereof I greet you in **Friendship**, (gives grip of first rank) in **Caution**, (gives grip of second rank) in **Bravery**, (gives grip of third rank.) The Sign of recognition or Challenge Sign is:

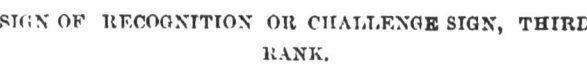

SIGN OF RECOGNITION OR CHALLENGE SIGN, THIRD RANK.

Place left hand over the heart; right hand open, palm down and about the height of the hips, indicating the position your hands were in when you took the obligation.

The answer is the same, indicating the same, it being simply the position your hands were in when assuming the obligation of the First, or **Initiatory** Rank of Page.

The Voting Sign is:

VOTING SIGN.

Clench the left hand and raise it about as high as the eyes.

The Semi-Annual Password, as its name indicates. and which is given at the outer door, (the Rank Passwords are not,) is*—

The Parry Sign is:

PARRY SIGN.

Bring sword to a "Present" and swing point from right to left as if to parry or ward off a blow. When sign is completed the right hand will be about a foot from the body and the sword will point about two feet in front of left foot.

---

*The Semi-Annual Pass Word from July 1878 to Jan 1879 was "*Be United.*"

The Grand Honors are given thus:

GRAND HONORS.

Place the left hand on the heart and sword at a " present."

SUPREME HONORS.

Given like Grand Honors except that left forearm is held horizontal, extending directly forward, elbow at side, with hand open and palm up.

Chancellor Commander.—"Keeper of Records and Seal, you will now present the roster of this Lodge to our Brother Knight John Brown for enrollment.

[Which being done, the Chancellor Commander says:]

Chancellor Commander.—"Master at Arms, you will now face the newly charged Brother Knight to the Lodge, and clothe him in the proper regalia or insignia of the Third, Chivalric and Honorable Rank of Knight." (Master at Arms does so.)

Master at Arms.—"Chancellor Commander, your orders have been obeyed."

Chancellor Commander (two raps).—"Officers, members and visitors of —— Lodge, No. —, Knights of Pythias, permit me to introduce to you Brother Knight John Brown, who has been regularly initiated in the First, Initiatory or Page, proved in the Second, Amorial or Esquire's, and fully charged in the Third, Chivalric, or Knight's Rank of this Order, in the usual ritualistic and ceremonial, [examined in accordance with the law—should such be the case], and enrolled as a member of —— Lodge, No. —, Knights of Pythias.

"Brethren, join with me in extending a hearty, sincere and chivalric welcome to our Brother Knight." (Mask is taken off.)

Chancellor Commander (one rap).—"Lodge will be at ease until the sound of the gavel at the Chancellor Commander's station."

[All gather around and shake hands.]

OFFICIAL VISITATIONS.

FORM OF CEREMONIALS TO BE USED IN SUPREME OR GRAND OFFICIAL VISITATIONS.

The Supreme or Grand Officer, being accompanied by (some one qualified to act as) the Supreme or Grand Guide enter the ante room in the regular way, when, after clothing themselves in the proper regalia or insignia of their rank, the Guide goes to the inner door and works his way into the Lodge in the ordinary manner, when, after the sign is taken up by the Chancellor Commander, or presiding officer, the Guide, while standing at the Altar, says:

Supreme Guide.—"Chancellor Commander, as the Supreme (or Grand, as the case may be) Guide, I am here to inform you that the Supreme (or Grand)—give the rank of the officer—is in waiting in the ante room, preparatory to making an official visitation to this Lodge.* You will therefore have your Lodge in readiness and instructed to give him the proper honors due his office when entering the Lodge."

Chancellor Commander (standing).—"Supreme (or Grand) Guide, in the name of this Lodge I thank you for your courteous notification, and will see that the proper honors are given."

The Guide then gives the countersign and retires. When the Lodge is ready the Guide is notified by the Guide of the Lodge, who comes out for that purpose and then goes in again. The Guide and Officer go to the inner door and give the proper alarm.

Inner Guard (raises the wicket and says in a loud voice).— "Who comes here?"

Guide.—"The Supreme (or Grand) Guide, accompanied by the (naming the officer), in his official capacity for visitation."

The Inner Guard closes the wicket and reports it to the Vice Chancellor; the Vice Chancellor, rising, reports it to the Chancellor Commander.

Chancellor Commander.—"It is my order as Chancellor Commander, that you admit them without further challenge."

Vice Chancellor (to Inner Guard).—"Brother Inner Guard, it is the order of the Chancellor Commander that you admit them without further challenge."

(Inner Guard opens the door and they enter.)

---

*If the Visiting Officer is a detailed one, his Guide will, at this point, read his commission as such, and in case he comes without a Guide, he may call into service any Past officer or competent member to act as such for him.

Chancellor Commander (two raps).—"Brethren, assist me in giving the Grand (or Supreme) honors."

All do so, the Guide and Officer going to the Altar, give the proper sign of the rank, which is responded to by the Chancellor Commander, when the Guide escorts the Visiting Officer to the Chancellor Commander's station, at his right hand; the Chancellor Commander hands the Officer the gauntlet—or gavel of authority, who takes it and orders "Recover," when the honors are dropped—or swords brought to a carry—and if armed, says, "Return swords," then gives three raps, when all are seated, the Supreme or Grand Guide in a chair at the right of the Lodge Master at Arms, when the object of the visit is explained and gone into. When ready to retire, he delivers the gavel to the Chancellor Commander, who accepts, (and having been informed of their intention of retiring,) gives two raps and says:

Chancellor Commander.—"Brethren, assist me in giving the Supreme (or Grand) honors," and the Supreme or Grand Officer, accompanied by his Guide, goes to the Altar—while the honors are being given, gives countersign and retires, when the Chancellor Commander orders, "Recover!" "return swords!" and seats the Lodge in the usual manner.

Remarks on Amplified Third Rank.

The essential part of the ceremonies of each rank is the OBLIGATION.

In each rank the candidate is asked whether or not he is willing to take a solemn and binding obligation to keep forever secret the mysteries of the rank.

"Let me read it first?" The candidate might reasonably reply. "I am commanded to prove all things in the Book of Law, the Holy Bible." (1 Thess. 5. 21.)

"No! you cannot; but I as Chancellor Commander assure you that it will in no wise affect your religion or your politics."

"What guarantee have I that your assurance is good? You wear your title by virtue of the votes of men who have dishonored the God of truth by not confessing His Son, and the Bible warns us not to trust in man".

"Thus saith the Lord: Cursed be the man that trusteth in man." Jer. 17: 5

"When the Lord shall stretch out his hand, both he that helpeth shall fall and he that is holpen shall fall down, and they all shall fail together." Isaiah 31 : 3.

"I must read the Obligation first, no prudent business man would sign a paper without first reading it." "The prudent man looketh well to his going." Prov. 14: 15.

"We have all taken the oath. You know us, if you cannot conform to our usages you may retire."

The obligations are Oaths; oaths hid from the candidate except as he takes their requirements upon himself; and, "If a soul swear pronouncing with his lips to do evil or to do good, whatsoever it be that a man shall pronounce with an oath and it be hid from him; when he knoweth of it, then *he shall be guilty* in one of these." Leviticus 5 ; 14.

Whether, then, the obligations of the Knights of Pythias are bad or good each person taking them can here read the Divine verdict upon the act "Guilty."

However, with this exposition in hand the oaths are not hid from us, and we have an opportunity to compare them with God's Word. The readers of this ritual can judge successfully whether or not the obligations conflict with the politics or religion of a Christian patriot, a person who recognizes God in Christ as the ruler of the state and also of the church.

The first paragraph of each oath binds to absolute secrecy during life from all but a small though miscellaneous set of men, concerning the mysteries (passwords, grips, signs, etc.,) of the Knights of Pythias.

If you are not a Christian, The Book of Law, God's Holy Word "*Now* commandeth all men everywhere to repent." Acts 17: 30. Christ says "come unto me." Matt. 11: 28. "Turn ye: turn ye." Ezekiel 33: 11.

The fact that you are a rebellious child does not release you from Christ's requirements. Give up your rebellion.

Christ says: "Follow me," Matt. 16: 24; 4: 19; 9: 9, 19: 21. Luke 18: 22; 5: 27; 9: 59. John 12: 26; 21: 22; 1: 43. And no one can follow Christ in combining with a number of fellowmen in the concealment of matters of pretended or general interest. Christ "spake openly to the World." He says: "In secret have I said nothing " John 18:20.

Friend, the Book of Law shows that the first part of each obligation comes into direct antagonism with your duty. The assurance of the Chancellor Commander to the contrary notwithstanding.

How men can be Republicans in sentiment and yet take vows of obedience to an irresponsible despotic aristocracy in secret lodges is a strange anomaly.

That such a rash vow is often repented at leisure the fact that forty-three thousand Knights in the State of Pennsylvania out of forty-five thousand, broke it by refusing obedience to an edict of the Grand Lodge, thus incurring, if the obligation is binding, the fearful self-imposed penalty of suffering all the anguish and torments possible for man to suffer, shows.

It is an historical fact that the Knights of the Dark Ages used to obtain oaths of persons by false pretenses and then make their dupes believe it to be their duty to fulfil them. A practice which gave rise to fearful abuses.

But in the darkness of this modern Knighthood there is a gleam of light. The Knights do not in the obligations fulfil their assurance of non-interference with the politics and religion of the candidate, and since they fail in fulfilling their part of the agreement, of course the covenant is void.

Still those taking these oaths are guilty. They have sinned by taking obligations that were hid from them, see Leviticus 5: 4—6; and also in promising to obey obligations at variance with the will of Christ as revealed in the Bible. And a person who finds himself in this sad condition should confess his sin. "He shall confess that he hath sinned in one of these." "If we confess our sins; he is faithful and just to forgive us our sins, and to cleanse us from all unrighteousness." 1 John 1: 9.

"He that covereth his sins shall not prosper: but whoso confesseth and forsaketh them shall have mercy." Prov. 28: 13.

The amplified form of the third rank, we believe no right minded person can read without horror. In the face of God's commands against swearing, unpremeditated profanity is awful; but words fail us when we contemplate a system which puts oaths into its regular order of exercises. The personification of Pluto the God of the infernal regions, (Satan) might be expected in such an assembly. And when the Knights who practice the amplified form of initiation, have concluded their demoniacal rites and "attend" while the prelate implores the blessing of Deity on their deliberations, can we avoid the fearful conclusion that the god of the lower regions rather than the dishonored, disobeyed, insulted Lord of the Holy Bible, attends and accepts their worship?

"I say, that the things which the Gentiles sacrifice, they sacrifice to devils and not to God: and I would not that ye should have fellowship with devils. Ye cannot drink the cup of the Lord and the cup of devils; ye cannot be partakers of the Lord's table and of the table of devils." 1 Cor. 10: 20-21.

"Have no fellowship with the unfruitful works of darkness, but rather reprove them, for it is a shame even to speak of those things which are done of them in secret." Eph. 5: 11-12.

"Woe unto them that call evil good, and good evil, that put darkness for light, and light for darkness." Isaiah 5: 20.

"Let the wicked forsake his way and the unrighteous man his thoughts; and let him return unto the Lord, and he will have mercy upon him; and to our God for he will abundantly pardon." Isaiah 55: 7.

"Then spake Jesus again unto them, saying: I am the light of the world; he that followeth me shall not walk in darkness, but shall have the light of life." John 8: 12.

KNIGHTS OF PYTHIAS AT A GLANCE.

FIRST OR INITIATORY RANK.

The preparation of the candidate in this Rank consists in removing the coat and vest, putting on a WHITE ROBE and blindfolding Securely. The members all have BLACK ROBES AND MASKS.

SIGN OF FRIENDSHIP OR COURTESY.

Form a link with the second finger of each hand, the back of the left hand up and the back of the right hand forward; the forearms forming the base of a triangle. [See cut.]

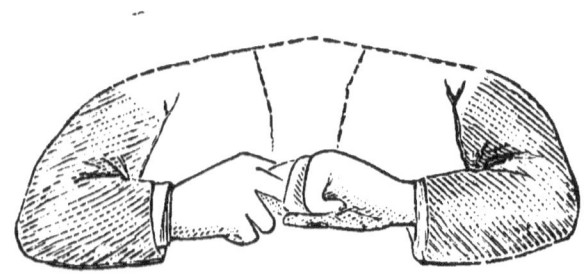

"The sign of Friendship or Courtesy, is always used on entering or retiring from the Lodge when open in the Rank of Page. It is recognized by the Chancellor Commander by giving the same sign or by a waive of the hand."

THE SIGN OF RECOGNITION.

Is given thus: Place your right thumb near the end of your two first fingees of same hand as though holding a pen to write, then smooth the hair back over the right ear with the two fingers, nails next to the head, three times, and is answered by the person saluted with the left hand in same manner.

INAUDIBLE SIGN OF CAUTION.

Raise right hand and with thumb and fore-finger squeeze the wings of the nose. This is done three times, noiselessly, in quick succession drawing the hand six or eight inches from the nose after each squeeze.

AUDIBLE SIGN OF CAUTION.

Made in the same way as Inaudible Sign, but to attract attention give a quick snuff each time as thumb and finger are being withdrawn from the nose.

ANSWER.—Same as Sign.

SIGN OF DISTRESS.

Strike the hands together three times, right hand uppermost.

There is a hailing word in connection with the Sign of Distress, which is **nomad,** (Damon back-wards).

ANSWER.—**Damon.**

GRIP, FIRST RANK.

Each extend the right hand, opening the fingers between the second and third as shown in upper cut, and grasp each others first two fingers, closing the other fingers as shown in lower cut.

WORD OR COVER KEY TO GRIP.

The Chancellor Commander and Master at Arms holding each other by the grip engage in the following colloquy:

Chancellor Commander.—"Say what is this?"
Master at Arms.—   "A good thing."
Chancellor Commander.—"Most people would say so."
Master at Arms.—   "Some would."
Chancellor Commander.—"O, would they?"
Master at Arms.—   "No doubt."

SECOND, OR RANK OF ESQUIRE.

PREPARATION.

The Page or Pages are taken to the ante-room in ordinary dress, and each one given a shield, which he is required to put on his left forearm, and from thence to the door of the Lodge, on the outside of which is suspended a shield, on which the Master at Arms gives **one** rap."

SIGN OF CAUTION OR COURTESY, RANK OF ESQUIRE.

Place right elbow in left hand and gently clinch the chin with the right hand. (See cut.)

COUNTERSIGN IN ANSWER: Same or a wave of the hand by the Chancellor Commander.

THE ALARM: One rap.

SHIELD SIGN.

Raise right hand perpendicularly, with the hand clinched as if in the act of striking a downward blow. Same position as when taking the obligation of this rank. (see cut.)

GRIP, RANK OF ESQUIRE.

Grasp left hands, in ordinary way. No shake.

THIRD, OR RANK OF KNIGHT.

NOTE.—The Signs, Grip, Pass-word etc., of the Amplified Third Rank are the same.

The candidate is prepared in the same manner as in the Second Rank.

SIGN OF BRAVERY OR COURTESY, THIRD RANK.

Form a triangle with forearms extending horizontally from you, points of fingers and thumbs together and spread out; heel of hands about five inches apart. (See cut.) This is called the visor sign.

VISOR SIGN ON ENTERING LODGE.

On entering to salute the Chancellor Commander, raise visor so as to touch the breast with the forefingers, the thumbs pointing downward. Hands are then separated and with a gentle wave are brought to the side.

VISOR SIGN ON RETIRING FROM LODGE.

On retiring approach the Altar, face the Chancellor Commander and turn the visor (hands) down, so that the thumbs point up and the fingers down and then bring hands to side with a gentle wave.

The Countersign, given by the Chancellor Commander, is same as sign or a wave of the hand. The Pass-word, given at the inner door, is **Confidence.** The Alarm at the inner door is two raps.

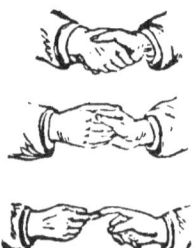

GRIP, THIRD RANK.

Take each other by the right hand as for ordinary hand shake. When withdrawing hands press each other's forefinger with thumb and forefinger, gently, the whole length of finger, slightly crooking the ends of the forefingers and hooking or **pressing** them together at the points.

SIGN OF RECOGNITION OR CHALLENGE SIGN.

Place left hand over the heart; right hand open, palm down and about the height of the hips, indicating the position your hands were in when you took the obligation.

The answer is the same, indicating the same, it being simply the position your hands were in when assuming the obligation of the First, or Initiatory Rank of Page.

VOTING SIGN.

Clench the left hand and raise it about as high as the eyes.

SEMI-ANNUAL PASS WORD.

The Semi-Annual Password, as its name indicates, and which is given at the outer door, (the Rank Passwords are not,) is*—

PARRY SIGN.

Bring sword to a "present" and swing point from right to left as if to parry or ward off a blow. When sign is completed the right hand will be about a foot from the body and the sword will point about two feet in front of left foot.

---

*The Semi-Annual Pass Word for the last half of 1878 (July to Jan.) was "Be United."

GRAND HONORS.

Place the left hand on the heart and sword at a " present."

SUPREME HONORS.

Given like Grand Honors except that left forearm is held horizontal, extending directly forward, elbow at side, with hand open and palm up.